FIT THE CRIME

The Impossible Lie

CORINNE ARROWOOD

Published by Corinne Arrowood
United States of America
www.corinnearrowood.com

ISBN: 978-1-962837-00-2 (eBook)
ISBN: 978-1-962837-01-9 (Trade Paperback)
ISBN: 978-1-962837-02-6 (Hardcover)

Cover and Interior Design by Cyrusfiction Productions.

TABLE OF CONTENTS

A Special Note

The statistics of PTSD are staggering. Many of our Marines and soldiers come home entrenched in the horrors they experienced and the nightmares they cannot escape. If you know one of our heroes that might be suffering from PTSD, contact Wounded Warrior Project, National Center for PTSD, VA Caregiver Support Line at 888-823-7458.

The Impossible Lie

TICKET TO RIDE

*L*ife was spinning out of control. The past several weeks had seemed like a never-ending bad nightmare. The hows and the whys remained a head-scratcher. During deployment and on missions, there was no time or practicality to postulate the things that happened. The Corps gave the orders, and he performed with loyalty, precision, and respect, never once crossing his mind to question if it seemed logical or fair, right or wrong. He did as told—end of thought. This new set of circumstances, civilian life, offered no rhyme or reason and left him in an always compromised position. *Right, Commander,* he thought, *civilian life was not for everyone,* and perhaps he was part of the mass of everyone.

The driveway onto the compound created the ambiance of driving through a botanical garden, lush and tranquil. Javier continued to make a big deal out of Babe's bullet wound. Almost like kissing his ass; it was over the top as far as the Marine saw it. Maybe the bossman detected his manipulative technique was backfiring. Yeah, Babe felt guilty for many things, but none were what someone else might surmise. There was no shame about maiming his father, no guilt about eliminating a threat of any kind; no, he felt guilty he hadn't taken care of business with Chop from the onset when his gut was saying something wasn't right. Then considered, when they first entered his apartment, the unsettled feeling alerted him something was awry, yet he blew it off. Had he reacted to his instinct, he wouldn't be in the predicament he found himself in presently. Any guilt he felt had to do with not responding to his senses, preservation instincts, and duty of protecting those who couldn't defend themselves. He'd gotten sloppy one too many times, and this was the result of his folly.

The first thing on his agenda, once they were at the house, was getting in the shower and digging the bullet out. It wasn't deep, barely below the surface, probably from a ricochet; he could likely grab it if his hands weren't so big. Someone tiny like his Creole blossom could have snatched it out with ease. Her tapered, thin fingers were like delicate surgical equipment, whereas his digits were more like mechanics tools, bulky but powerful.

The front door opened as they approached the sprawling home. A young woman stood with a welcoming smile. She could have easily been one of the models posed in Sports Illustrated Swimsuit Edition or Playboy; she was intoxicatingly beautiful. "Welcome home." She nodded at Javier and then looked at Babe, "Welcome to Casa Garcia." Her full smile radiated warmth with heart-shaped lips and perfectly white teeth. The cleft in her chin was not too deep but enough to give her appearance a strong yet feminine presence.

"Carmen, please show Captain Vicarelli to his quarters and summon a physician to assist with his wound." She bowed her head politely and answered it would be her pleasure. Javier went in a different direction than she was pursuing. Babe tried to watch where he was going but lost sight of him once in a dramatic hall festooned with seemingly expensive pieces of art. As one could feel the nuance of fine furniture, such was the artwork displayed on the walls and sculptures in the corners. She attempted friendly small talk as she led him to his suite.

Javier didn't do anything half-assed. The focal point of the suite was a spectacular tropical view. From the apparent thickness of the glass, he figured it was shatterproof. The furnishings were first-rate, like his grandfather's, but not as heavy, more modern. The living area of his room had a rectangular fire pit inlaid into a coffee table that glowed with hues of brilliant turquoise and blue like a river setting off an ivory leather L-design sectional. Everything had a hint of the tropics, with soothing aquatic shades popped by brightly colored throw pillows. The bed was massive, king-size, and canopied, raised high off the floor, adorned with netting gathered on each of the four corner posts and across the top. Luxury at its finest. "Ma'am, I'll be getting in the shower; thank you for guiding me, but I can take it from here." Babe tried to say get out without being rude.

"Let me take your soiled clothing. You will find a robe in the closet," Carmen swept her hand toward a closed mirrored door. "Seignor Garcia will have suitable garments for you; he has already sent word, and you will have all you need within the next hour." She smiled with a slight tilt of her head, still not budging from where she stood.

If she wasn't going to leave without the dirty clothes, he had no problem disrobing. Being shy about his body had never been a thing. Babe kicked off his shoes, grabbed the knife from his sock, then dropped his damaged joggers and underwear, stripping the bullet-torn Henley over his head. He heard her hold a startled breath. *Look, but do not touch,* he thought. *Was it the wound or my body stifling her breath? Whatever. Trinity,* he recited in his heart, not that he needed a reminder.

She approached, and his eyes took on an unmistakable message to come no further. He balled the clothes and gently tossed them to her. "Gracias," he turned toward the bathroom, started the shower, and hung a towel over the glass door. Watery blood-tinged streaks flowed in streams forked with tributaries down his leg. All in all, the wound wasn't more than an exaggerated puncture in his mind. The shower spray made it look far worse than it was. Although his weapon was only a steak knife from the hotel, he inserted the point beneath the metal, and with a flick of the wrist, he popped it out like a fly ball. "Fuck!" He grimaced in discomfort, clenching his jaws.

Babe heard a knock on the door to his suite. "Yes? In the shower." A man cleared his throat outside the bathroom door. "Enter."

After rubbing his eyes, Babe focused on the person entering. Javier said, "I have the doctor to attend to your wound." The cartel man carried himself with an air of grace, not a thug-ness in his demeanor. Once again, looks could be deceiving.

3

"I got the bullet out, but I'm bleeding and don't wanna fuck up the rug and towel." Javier tossed a black towel over the shower door. *Hm.* The thought ran through his mind. *My peculiar host seems prepared for injured company, odd.* Babe dried off enough and held the towel tightly into the puncture to stifle the blood and ooze. "Ask him to leave a few bandages in the room, and I'll be fine." Using the other towel, he dried his face and stepped out of the shower, padding to the bedroom. Javier sat casually on the sofa. "Nice digs ya got here, sir." The doctor was still in the room. "Doc, I got this; just leave some tape and bandages." The physician was a tiny man; he looked similar to a few of Trinity's brothers but smaller. He smiled and held up a syringe. "What's that?"

"Antibiotic, you have allergy?" the physician asked in broken English.

Babe turned his hip to the man, unwrapping the black towel, exposing a viable injection site. "Go ahead." Once accomplished, Babe responded, "All good," he waved the doctor off, but the man pointed to the wound as though saying 'let me see.' He opened the towel again, pointing to the slight damage. The man nodded to Javier and gave a thumbs up. "I told ya, all's good. Gracias." The man left, and Babe sat on the chaise section of the sofa.

Javier handed the big man a stack of hundred-dollar bills secured by a band. "For your service as promised." Babe wanted to say he thought the reward was his life. He remembered *your loyalty or your life.* "Give yourself a few days to heal, and then if you wish to return home, I'll have my jet take you to New Orleans. I caution you to think long and hard about your decision." There wasn't much to think about. Javier's attempt at manipulating him came close to working, but he didn't succumb. Babe understood Javier's desire to keep him around, but what he didn't get was why Commander Deary was in bed with the cartel. The story of Marines falsely held smacked of bullshit. They would've fought to the death, not just pussied out and said, okay, I give up—an impossible lie, they were Marines. There was more to the story. Sure, Deary could have recommended him, but giving personal information was breaking trust, not the standards of a Marine.

Babe let loose with his questions. He wanted answers. "What happened to Seb? Where's Noir? Where's Deary? What strings are you trying to attach to me?" He held his tongue for a brief second and continued. "I don't like what you're organization does. It's something I would give my life to fight against. I'm not a fan of drug smuggling, but people make poor decisions. Drugging kids and sex trafficking is a whole different ball of wax. I see perversion like hurting kids, and I eliminate the offender with a clear conscience. Grown-ass men and women wanting to have sex with kids are fucking disgusting, and handling it as a money-making machine, those people need to be castrated with their dicks lobbed off. What's the deal? Can't they handle a grown woman or man? I've done a lot of fucking, but never once had any inclination to hose a kid, and as far as these teenage boys, you got a lot of sick motherfuckers for clients. What, you fancy yourself the Jeffrey Epstein of the cartel world? You might want to kill me now before I come after you. Food for thought, chief." He clicked his mouth and winked. "You saved my life, and I owed you a debt. I paid it. Make your money off something else, not kids, then you and me, we're good. I'll give it a few days, and then I want to go home, never to hear or see you again. We have a deal?"

Javier sat silently, absorbing everything Babe had said, calculating his response. "Even if I send you home, Deary is coming for you. See, Marine, you know too much about his secrets. You pick your poison. Get snaked by him for no money or earn money beyond your wildest dreams with me? Take a couple of days to decide. Being prepared to know your enemy is the best advice I can offer. We will talk again, but until then, rest. Carmen will bring you some food; I'm sure you are hungry. You can't use it now," pointing to his injury, "but I have a workout room that'll make your dick hard when you're ready. Your clothes should be here momentarily." He sat for a minute, watching for expression on the Marine's face. If he'd felt anything, he'd disguised it well. Javier stood, answered a call, and turned to Babe. "Talk later."

Carmen walked in with full bags draping off her arm as the boss walked out. Behind her was a younger girl with a tray of food in her hand; she placed it on the table and swiftly left. Babe jumped up to assist and audibly sucked air through his teeth, "Shit, I forgot, bad move," grabbing his side. He relieved Carmen of the bags. Babe couldn't help but notice her erect nipples through the fitted silky top. He speculated she was somewhere around five-six, without the heels. Her long black hair draped over her arms past her shoulder blades.

Carmen gasped, "Sir, you are bleeding again. Let me change your bandage for you." Before he could move or say no, she'd pulled the towel off him, using the corner to wipe the streak of blood trickling along his body. So close to the wound, he could feel her whispering breath slightly stir across his skin. It was enough to incite the blood racing in his body. His cock responded involuntarily. "Sir, I can help." She lightly passed her breasts against him. The warmth of her skin against his swollen member was more stimulation than he could take. He wanted to back away and stay faithful to Trinity, but the primal pulsing was more than he could bear. His shame did not stop the inevitable; it felt too good. In his mind, he pictured Trinity. While the moment was glorious physically, the guilt robbed him of any pleasure.

"Leave." He demanded. Babe was pissed, more at himself, but it fired straight at the girl. He didn't like the feeling; it tore at his gut, squeezing his heart, living the scenario over and over. Wasn't he man enough to control his body and, if not, at least have the balls to push her from him or step away? No, part of him wanted it; it was the only explanation.

HOUSE OF MEN

*B*abe reclined on the bed, watching Carmen quickly exit the room as he had requested, with her tail tucked between her legs and obvious hurt feelings. He hadn't meant for things to evolve as they had. Maybe this was his new life, and it was how it would have to be so Trinity could live the rest of her life without hindrance. He longed to look into her eyes, to hold her and have a happily-ever-after with her, but how would he ever explain what happened, not just the blow job, but agreeing to work with the cartel? Her idea of him as a superhero would flush down the drain, as it should. He was anything but a superhero.

Did I encourage the woman in any way? Did I send signals that I was open for play, or was this a setup by Javier? The thoughts zinged through like pelts of hard rain. Carmen wasn't a hooker or call girl, he easily surmised; if so, she hadn't mastered the knack. Unfortunately, he was all too familiar with call girls and their abilities. He figured if one does a hummer many times a day, three sixty-five, one should be proficient at sucking a golf ball through a hose. No, she was a beautiful girl with a lovely body and a caring way.

There was a knock. Babe, still wrapped in a towel, got up and answered. At his door was a boy, maybe five or six years old. In a barely intelligible accent, the child spoke, "Hello. For you from Papa. Yes?" It was an English Bible, worn and pliable, a stark contrast to the rigid unused book in the hotel room. "Gracias," one of the few words he knew. Why would Javier send him a Bible? Did the call girl from the hotel tell him? She had to. It was the only way.

The boy smiled and spoke, "You are very welcome."

Babe held up the Bible, "From your Papa, Mr. Garcia?" The boy's eyes twinkled as he joyfully nodded. "Gracias." The big guy repeated. The child giggled and ran away. While brief, there was a feeling of being lifted, like when he was at Bethany's speaking with Rainie but observing Trinity's nieces and nephews laugh and play. His heart pictured happiness, yet the feeling of loss cramped his chest, stifling his breath. *Will there ever be another time to watch them play? Will I one day enjoy Trinity's and my children play, or was it a done deal?*

There was a matter of unpacking the bags Carmen had brought to him. Once again, there were more clothes than necessary. Included in the shopping bag were a few pairs of lightweight lounge pants. He immediately grabbed one and slid them on. Any twisting or leaning movement shot pain straight to his gut, causing a wince. He stretched out on the bed carefully and opened the Bible, flipping to the last psalm and the verse he had repeated several times. "Let everything that has breath praise the Lord. Praise the Lord." (Psalms 150:6 NIV) He slammed the book closed. *Not for me.* His mind wouldn't let go, though.

While sorrowfully miserable, that one small moment with Javier's son brought joy; perhaps he needed to praise the Lord for the small blessing. It unleashed powerful emotions, making him more determined to get through whatever it was to get home to Trinity. *Okay, Trey and Trinity, I'm trying this God thing on. If there is a God, He'll return me home.* He picked up the book again, turned the page, and began a new chapter, Proverbs, which brought up memories of being in Africa.

Babe thought of his team in Africa. Nigel Hawkins, a Brit born with an American dad, was part of Babe's team and the chatty one of the group. He knew how to lift spirits and had a way with everyone while accomplishing their missions, frothed with horror and bleak circumstances. One of his favorite things was to make up quotes, saying, 'Confucius says,' then rattling off some ridiculous narrative hardly relevant to their pursuit but a much-needed distraction, especially with the prevalence of barbaric violence and inhumane atrocities in small villages in The Sudan.

The memory took front and center of his mind. The picture was clear, as though it was reality and not a flashback.

"Vic, help," he remembered hearing the raspy whisper from the other side of a spindly shrub. Peering to the other side, he saw the problem. Hurley's boot had snagged but, thankfully, not pulled a tripwire laid down from the previous unrest. He was trembling such that his movement could apply enough pressure to set it off.

"Hawkins, my six." The man moved with agility and stealth.

"Hurley, I got this. Don't move." Babe instructed.

Hawkins whispered, "Hurley, Confucius say, boy who trip wire sing soprano for the angels."

"Don't you laugh, Hurley. Hawk, no more Confucius." While his remarks generally settled the nerves, sometimes they induced laughter, which could be deadly for all three of them right then.

While the name proverbs conjured thoughts of Confucius, he knew the two had no connection but did bring a brief smile to his face, thinking of Nigel Hawkins. He was one of the lucky ones who made it out without injury or mental health issues; maybe Confucius kept him sane. His mind wondered where he ended up. How ashamed Babe would be for any of his team to see him now. Granted, he did what he had to do to stay alive; it certainly wasn't the actions of any honorable Marine.

Babe wanted to read more about David; he felt a connection with him for some odd reason. So he looked to the back, referencing David, finding his beginning in 1 Samuel. A couple of hours went by when there was a knock on the door. He got up and answered. He planned if it were Carmen, he would not let her in the room and tell her to go away. Yeah, guilt was riding him pretty hard; he shrugged because it should. There was no excuse; he had been pathetic and weak, but it wasn't the girl; it was Javier. Babe ushered him in. "Why are you staying locked up in this room? There is much to see and do here; you will find it is not such a terrible place."

Babe walked to the sofa and sat. "There are too many unanswered questions. I asked you before, where is Noir, what happened to Seb, Commander Deary, and what do you want from me?" He felt his muscles tighten as the fire in his gut smoldered with impatience and anger.

Javier sat, crossed his legs, and spread his arms across the top of the sofa—too comfortable and smug to register sincerity. Babe's respirations and pulse increased the angrier he became. "Isn't there something I can offer you that will calm your aggression? Your emotions are, how do you say it—"

"Fucking pissed off? Yes, sir, I am one angry motherfucker right now. You have been deceptive and most, as you spoke of your adversary, dishonest. I've been crystal clear with you from the get-go. You asked for my loyalty; I told you then, and I'll say it again: I do not know you well enough, yet I honored my word. You, sir, have not honored yours." Babe felt his jaw muscles tighten and the heat rising in his body. He'd like nothing more than to knock the shit out of the guy, so what if it meant his death. At this point, he felt dead already.

Javier brought his hands to rest as he leaned forward toward the Marine. "Answer one; Noir is, and he looked at his watch, probably more than halfway to Quebec. I think it is where he lives most of the time with his family. I hadn't seen him since we were boys. Actually, I met him through my friend Mateo, who worked at the same resort as Noir's mother and the boy; they were friendly, but he was an extremely shy, quiet boy. You see, Mat and I were like brothers," he crossed his fingers, displaying how connected he had been with his friend.

"I never knew much about Noir, but he was always pleasant. Occasionally, I would run into him, but then he moved away. He called me not long ago and asked if I knew of any work. It was a peculiar thing as I did not know him very well. He said he'd heard of Mateo's death then and meant to call but was very busy as head of security for a wealthy Canadian elite. He would not give me the name; evidently, the man passed of heart failure, and Noir was looking for similar work. I had my people check on any sudden deaths in the elite circles. His story checked out. One of my people found a picture of him.

"When I saw how menacing he appeared, I thought I knew just the right situation to test his loyalty and skills, which I won't get into now; unfortunately, loyalty in Cartagena is difficult to find. I needed someone not attached to the area. Everyone is always jockeying for power. He passed the first two tests of loyalty, so I thought he'd be ideal for protection but needed another independent." He stood, went to the small refrigerator in the wet bar, and opened a bottle of Perrier.

Javier paced in front of the window, commenting on how beautiful his paradise was. Did Babe not agree? Still clad in loungewear, he tipped his head. One couldn't argue; it was magnificent, beautiful hardly described the splendor, but it might as well have been a jail cell; he felt imprisoned. "So Noir is returning to his family?" Babe asked, and Javier nodded.

"Yes, he is, for now. I have another detail for him in a few months, and he is returning. I have encouraged him to bring his family, and I would have a house built for them on the compound."

"And you'd make the same offer to me? I can fly Trinity here?" Babe tilted his head.

Javier shook his head with furrowed brows. "No. Her father would not allow her to move from him. Mr. Noelle is a powerful man, and I do not need to quarrel with him; we have different business interests." He sat, angling his body toward Babe. "Seb. You asked about him. He is young, astute, and loyal, but he is not someone to be head of my security. He works well with the more corporate side of things, which I thought I might need in the past meeting, but no." He turned up one hand. "You saw how well that worked." He put his bottle on the table and rubbed his forehead as though thinking or catching the beginning of a headache.

It was Babe's turn to get up and grab a bottle of water, just regular, not sparkling. He leaned against the wet bar and asked, "And Commander Deary?" He settled with a long exhalation.

Javier reclined against the back of the sofa, "I'm afraid it is a hard one. I told you already how he and Mat met, and I called upon him. Otherwise, you'd be dead. You interfered with my business and cut off a lucrative operation; there is but one answer to such a problem. When I found out it was a one-man show and it happened to be the one person Deary would trust, well, as they say, the rest is history." He leaned forward again, this time splaying his fingers. "This is where it gets dicey. You know now about the Commander's connection to me. I am certain your Marine Corps would not be happy with the interaction. If he were CIA, eh, it would be no big deal." He shrugged. "It is commonplace. I feel certain the Commander will erase you, maybe not if you got to him first, but—" he moved his hands, flipping them back and forth, palm up, palm down, "Comme Ci, Comme Ca. You get him; he gets you; could you eliminate your hero?" Javier cocked his head.

Babe retaliated in a curt tone of voice, "Could you have assassinated Mateo Moreno? Every time you mention his name, I can see it ding your soul. Could you?"

Javier kicked the coffee table, and it slid a good three feet. "It is nowhere near the same thing," he growled. *Interesting, his Achille's Heel,* Babe reflected.

Babe walked behind Javier and patted his shoulder, "No insult meant." He walked around and sat. "Commander Deary? It would be hard, but could I do it? Fuck, yeah. It'd sting, no lie, but I could do it in a heartbeat to have my life back to the way it was. It would be tricky because the man is rarely alone. Now the final question, will you allow me to return to my home, no strings attached?"

Javier stood, "You must come out of this room and see what it is like to live here, but to answer you, yes, I will provide safe passage home for you on the one condition: if I need you again, you will make yourself available. Think about it, and for fuck sake, put some clothes on, stop pouting, and come see."

"Gunnnner!" The dog yipped and jumped in rapturous joy. She could almost hear him saying, 'She's here; oh boy, she's back.' He went behind her as though looking for something. The something was Babe. *And they say dogs have no memory after a few days, no sense of time. Bullshit!* "Hey, my boy. Sorry, he's not back yet." Trinity stared off, thinking, *will he ever be back?*

She heard her mother back in the bedroom. "Honey, I knew you were almost home, nearly a block away. Gunner is some kind of smart. He misses you when you're not here."

The Noelles decorated their home tastefully with a modern touch mixed with the odd antique here and there. When she and her siblings were younger and growing up in the house, it had colorful walls and was comfortable with sturdy furniture, considering the five boys, but it was still lovely. Since all the kids had grown and left the house, her mother remodeled it to a sleeker, vogue look. Everything was white and gray with a touch of color from massive floral arrangements and a pillow or two. It was a big house with over six thousand square feet. She remembered walking to the lakefront, smoking cigarettes, and being all cool while the breeze off the lake blew her hair in all directions.

Swan Street had three large families like hers, so finding playmates was never a problem. Thinking about her teenage years, she had been boy-crazy since turning ten, and by twelve, she had kissed some of the neighborhood boys. On the other hand, Bethany rarely glanced in the direction of a boy and acted subdued and studious. They were as opposite as possible but closer than a tick on a dog.

Trinity checked out all the family photos from their childhood as well as the weddings of Neville, Charles, and Louis, which her mom had scattered throughout the house. It reminded her of Babe's photos on his walls. Everyone had pictures, while she had none, emphasizing the point she didn't have one with Babe. First thing when he got back, she determined they were going to get professional pictures done. The tears began to fall, and the squeeze of her heart was painful. She called to her mother. "Mama, quick." The expression on her mother's face was of horror. "I think I'm having a heart attack. It hurts so bad right here," pointing to her sternum. "Mama, I can hardly breathe. Oh, my God." Her mother hugged her, stroking her hair. She led Trinity into the kitchen, wet a dishtowel, and held it on her wrists.

"Baby girl, you're not having a heart attack, maybe an anxiety attack, but definitely not your heart. I'm not saying it doesn't feel that way. What were you thinking about, baby?"

Trinity broke down, sobbing; she didn't have a single picture of Babe and none of the two of them together. "I can't live without him, Mama." Her mother quieted her while Gunner put his head on her lap.

Babe dressed and explored the house. There was laughter and loud cracks as the stripes and solids smacked into each other in a game of pool. The house rambled forever, and he followed the sound. The game room overlooked a terrace with giant columns. The backyard, if one could call it a yard, was lavish, with a pool the size of one at a resort. The grounds were park-like. In the yard were several men trimming the manicured gardens comprised of vivid flowers and lush greens. Three women clad in bikinis played with four children in the pool—one boy and three girls, all with black hair and deep olive skin. The boy who came to his room with the Bible was nowhere in sight, nor was Carmen. *Interesting,* he thought.

Seb patted Babe on the shoulder. "Welcome to Casa Garcia. A beautiful site to behold, wouldn't you agree?"

Staring off into space, he asked, "Whose kids? I don't see Javier's son. Are any of those women his wife?" Seb laughed like the question was funny. He answered the women were girlfriends of some of the guys, and Little Javi and Angelina, Javi's kids, were with the tutor. Maria, Javier's wife, and her sister Carmen were planning the menu for the week. Babe asked, "Carmen is Javier's sister-in-law?" *Well, doesn't that beat all? What a bizarre world it was in Cartagena. Maybe the girl wasn't a setup by Javier, but what would the consequences be of the private incident?*

Seb did a double raise of his eyebrows. "Muy hermoso. Um, very beautiful and completely taboo." *Oh shit!* Babe closed his eyes for a second and slowly shook his head. "I know, man, like, why bring her here to the house of men if she's a look but don't touch? Let me show you around."

They headed to the pool and a pathway leading to a smaller house. "Who lives there?"

"We gotta be quiet, man. The night crew is sleeping." They silently passed the house. Further onto the property were two more beautiful homes, nowhere as big as Javier's but still quite large. "Hopefully, this will be mine one day," Seb pointed to one. "Right now, it's empty. The other one is Maria and Carmen's mother. Carmen stays there, too, but no sneaking around, man. There are cameras and guards everywhere. Javier would skin you alive." *It just keeps getting better,* he thought sarcastically. The path circled back to the pool and main house, but in the far back of the property, Babe could see the roof of a metal building.

"What's back over there?" Babe pointed to the back of the property. Suddenly, the man seemed uncomfortable and nervous.

"Probably lawn equipment, but don't go back there. Here, come this way." Seb showed Babe the kitchen, the dining area, and then back into the game room. "Javier has an office near his bedroom down that hall and, once again, off limits." The hallways were like three spokes on a wheel. One was to the guest quarters, which he was more than familiar with; one was for his children and the nanny, and the third was Javier and Maria's room with a connecting study. "Usually, no women are in the house, but Maria and Carmen are back from traveling to Spain. They are almost always gone; it's why we call it a house of men. Even the cook is a man, and the cleaning crew is as well. There's a lotta testosterone here, and the fights don't end in fists; people get loco, pulling out knives and guns. When are you leaving?" He stood with his hands on his hips.

Babe scratched his head, "Very good question, sir. I have no idea. Javier told me to make a list of things I needed. I don't have paper, a pen or a phone. Can you find me a phone?"

Seb raised his shoulders with up-turned hands, then pulled out his phone. "Javi, sorry to bother you. The big guy wants a phone. Will do." He smiled at Babe, who was expecting a no-dice on the phone. He stood awkwardly with his hands in his pockets as the conversation briefed. "Boss says, get something to eat, and I'll get you a phone with an internet password installed. Oh, no locking the phone. He checks them occasionally. Because it's unannounced and not routine, he's caught a couple of men texting another cartel." He briskly shook his head. "Ugly," he drew in a rattled breath. Babe thought *any idea what I'm capable of? You'd shit your pants or puke.* Seb opened a drawer and handed Babe a pen and paper.

Seb led the way immediately into the kitchen and asked the cook, he supposed, for food—anything would be good. He left Babe in pursuit of a phone. "I'm Vicarelli, and you?"

"Bernard." Babe smiled while thinking, *Bernard? Not Miguel or Carlos?* "Go sit." He remembered where the dining room was and sat at the table. Seb came in fiddling with a new phone.

"It's ready to go. Already charged." He left the room.

Babe texted: It's me. I love you. Gonna need another haircut. LOL.

Trinity: Sweet Jesus. Can I call you?

Babe: You can try.

He took a bite just as the phone rang; he swallowed fast. "Trinity?" He felt the mist coating his eyes and a lump swell in his throat.

"Babe?" She started to cry.

"Don't cry, Trinity. Now you have a number to reach me. I don't know when I'm coming home. There's something I gotta do before seeing you."

"Please come home. I love you."

"As soon as I can. I love you, too, ma girl." He didn't want to hang up, but there was no reason to torture her or himself. He had a loose end that needed tying.

ONE WAY

*B*abe let two days go by plotting the how and when to take out Commander Deary. Dirty cops were a blight, but a dirty Marine Commander was disgraceful, nothing short of puke-worthy, and twisted his gut just thinking about it. The position's power and control made the rank the closest thing to a god in his eyes. While the Commandant was the top dog, the bureaucracy and the way of politics never put them in contact with their Marine boots on the ground save some stupid pomp and circumstance, which was nothing more than a circle-jerk. People's lives lay in the balance of the decisions they made, and Deary was a traitor.

Looking back, he doubted Yuhn was a treasonist or terrorist, but Babe followed the order and eliminated the threat. He'd questioned the Commander back then, but Deary reminded him it wasn't his to contest but to follow command. His job was to obey orders, not expect explanations. He had looked up to the man and held him in the highest esteem. Deary was one of those people who commanded stoically but always let his Marines know he was there for them. The Commander would not be an easy target, and once Javier let him know Babe was homebound, he was sure he'd try some underhanded maneuver, now knowing the nature of the man.

Babe googled information on Hotel Noelle. There was a selection for reservations, directions, rates, and contact. If he selected contact, would it probably go to some corporate reservation switchboard or connect straight to the hotel? He couldn't risk it. He didn't want to ask Trinity for her dad's number because it would only create a whirlwind of questions. Babe needed to know Trinity was safe, and he felt the only one able to guarantee her safety was Antoine Noelle. He looked up Louie's and called.

Samantha answered the phone. "Louie's Tap." Just the sound of her voice was annoying, like a nasally whine. She thought she was the sexiest thing on two legs, *wrong*.

"Nathan Shephard, please."

"Who's calling?" He heard the snapping of her gum and could visualize her stance, expression, and twirling of her hair around her finger.

"George Rune. I'm calling from out of the country. Get him on the line, miss."

She put her hand over the phone and yelled to a name he didn't recognize to get Shep.

A minute later, a gruff voice came over the phone. "You got him." A heavy breath echoed into Babe's ear.

"Don't say anything, Shep. This is Babe." Immediately, he heard Shep about to comment; knowledge spelled disaster. "No, just listen. Act like it's a business call, and for Pete's sake, don't tell anyone you've spoken to me. I've talked to ma girl, but not even her, okay?"

"I got it."

"What is the number for Antoine's direct line?" He heard Shep blow out a studdered breath. It was apparent he was uncomfortable and hesitant. Babe put him in an awkward situation.

"You know, I wouldn't ask if it wasn't important. Antoine won't know you gave me his number. I've called him before. I wouldn't ask, but I don't have my phone; this is a loaner." He knew there was urgency in his voice, with due cause.

"Shit. Okay, here's the number. Got a pen?" Babe answered yes and jotted the number.

"You are literally a lifesaver. Thanks. Later."

Babe had to figure out the right words to say to Antoine, to let him know the pressing consequences and danger without alarming him. He rehearsed it in his mind. Five minutes later, Babe placed the call.

"Antoine Noelle," the man answered in a professional but pleasant voice.

"Sir, this is Babe Vicarelli. I have to be quick, and I need you to listen to what I say."

"You've got my attention, Marine."

"I'm returning to the States in two days. There is a man coming to kill me or try to, and I need Trinity safe. He will use her to get to me as leverage. She will fight you on this, but if you let her know I've asked, she might not kick up as much. I'd rather her not be at your home, but maybe stay at the hotel or a safe house if you have one, definitely not her apartment. Do you have someone you trust enough to stay with her and keep her safe? It would be best to keep the appearance of business as usual. I've got to kill this guy before he kills me, and time will be of the essence."

"I understand. Can I handle the matter for you?"

"No, sir. Even you can't reach him. I have to. So, not tomorrow, but the next day, you need to act swiftly. Can I count on you?"

"Absolutely. She's my baby girl. You may love her, but I loved her first. Good luck, and if you need my help, call."

"I did, sir. Knowing she's in your protection eliminates my main concern, and I got it from here."

****

Back in Metairie, Trinity's friends, who provided information on Babe's situation following the abduction, chatted back and forth. "Michael, have you heard any more from William? Is Babe out of the woods yet? I can't help but think of poor Trinity. I hated it when you had those secret Mateo surgery trips, and that was only over a weekend. Plus, I knew what you were doing and who you were with, kinda. She must be going bonkers." She watched him as he stood in front of the mirror, flipping his tie around into the perfect knot. "Do the other partners wear a tie? Like is it in some manual or rule book? I think ya'll would be cute in scrubs with a logo." He chuckled at her never-ending stream of questions and out-the-box comments while her eyes admired his butt.

If he had to bet, the next question to come out of her mouth would be about a butt lift. Nothing was wrong with her butt; in fact, she had a great ass especially being as thin as she was. He loved his wife, and as far as he was concerned, she was the most gorgeous creature in the world.

"I'll check in with Mateo, um, William. Sound good? Remember, I have a staff meeting today; I'll see what my partners think about the idea of scrubs. As it is, Rai, we wear jeans on Friday. What would we do on dress down Friday? Come in our drawers?" He gave her a quick kiss and headed down the stairs, knowing she was a step behind him.

On the way to the office, he called William. "Bonjour Mike. How is my favorite surgeon today? Business good? I suppose you are interested in any news."

"Yes, you are indeed correct; you know Rainie." He flipped the turning indicator as he approached the expressway ramp from Metairie Road.

"It seems your Marine has fallen into good graces, and Javi offered him a position in the organization. He does not take to people so easily; your friend must be impressive."

"He is; think of the Terminator if you've seen the movie."

"I cannot say I have, but I understand the gist. My contact has returned home, and I now cannot be of any assistance. We are both blind. I am certain the offer Javier made is a handsome one. How motivated is your friend by money and position? That will indicate the future."

"What I can tell is neither money nor position is his motivator. Thank you, my friend."

"Take care, Mike."

Babe watched a close game of eight-ball. No doubt, Casa Garcia was a house of men, and for the most part, he had no idea what the men lounging in the game room were chattering about, nor did he care. Their conversation was entirely in Spanish. He watched their body language, figuring out the pecking order. With their bravado, it was easy to peg the order. All went silent, and when Babe looked to his left, he saw Javier and Seb had entered the room.

"Glad to see you out of your quarters, Marine." The bossman said, walking up. "Do we have anything to talk about? Have you decided on a plan?" There was no doubt Javier had a transmitter lodged in the cell phone and heard all of his conversations. There was no point in lying.

Babe stood with one hand on the injured hip, perhaps an unconscious protection mechanism. "I spoke with my girl and told her I'd be coming home soon." He looked Javier directly in the eyes. "No set date, but I did tell her father to find a safe place for her. Now, the question for you. Are you going to notify the Commander when I leave and where I'll be landing? Am I to expect an ambush?" Javier stood calmly and listened but shook his head no.

"Come to my study." Babe followed as Javier and Seb entered what he called the Bossman Hall. Javier seemed to glide as he walked, still and poised, unlike Seb, who had the gangster young man's exaggerated strut, like he thought he was all that. All the guy was lacking was the baseball hat under a hoody. Babe wasn't judging, merely observing; in fact, one of his favorite clothing items was his sleeveless hoody back home. Seb came across as young, too young to have a weighty responsibility, but then again, he had many a Marine under his command, too young to be in the warzone. Babe followed while they spoke to each other. Like a good assistant or lieutenant, Seb scribbled as his boss instructed.

They turned into a doorway on the right, "Seb, go entertain yourself with the guys, our guest and I are fine by ourselves and shut the door on your way out." Babe felt the icy glare from the young man in his peripheral vision. Body language spoke volumes if one bothered to pay attention. Javier was a cool customer, not demonstrating any sign of emotion, but so was Babe. They were similar in their demeanor—quiet, observant, and intense. "I have no plans to speak with your Commander Deary unless I need another bodyguard stud, but Noir has assured me I can call upon him. And you?"

Silence. Babe had to think that one through. If, perchance, he was to return to the military or work for Antoine, beck and call for anyone else would be out of the question. "I don't know. I have several options to consider, which in some ways is good, but it can be perplexing for a Marine who functions at high levels through commands. I have weighed staying here, but it's not my lifestyle. Working at a low-paying construction site, which, by the way, is better than low-paying, not what you have offered for sure, but I'm a simple man requiring little, and there's always going back to the Marines. They liked me." He threw a cocky grin.

They discussed the options. Javier paid close attention to Babe's words. He didn't have a comment on returning to the construction job, raised his eyebrows at the thought of the Marine working for Antoine, but hearing about re-enlisting in the military caused him to clear his throat, almost choking. "You do realize, Captain Vicarelli—"

"Babe." He corrected.

"Babe, you'd be signing your own death warrant. I doubt you would make it through whatever training you might have. A misfire from another Marine, a wildly thrown knife to the neck, poison; there are many options." The man looked honestly concerned, his forehead rippled and eyebrows furrowed together. "I know you are an intelligent and well-read man, plus I have seen you in action." Javier applauded with three claps of his hands. "Truly remarkable, indeed, but you would be walking into the lion's den, spider's web, call it what you may. No way you come out on top." He raised an eyebrow, shaking his head slowly. "I can't fathom one scenario if you re-enlisted where you wouldn't be dead inside a few days if not hours."

Hm. Babe sat quietly, trying to use the appropriate words, and then it came to him. "There's a bit of advice I heard once in a movie, and it rang true—keep your friends close but your enemies closer. It's a good theory; like know your enemy as you suggested." Javier rocked his head from side to side, extending his bottom lip in consternation.

"Drink?" he asked.

"Two-finger pour of whiskey, please." Javier poured the beverages and raised his glass.

"May we meet again as friends!" Babe nodded, all the while thinking the conversation had been too easy. The bossman had not made much of a rebuttal and made a point to say he was not going to contact Deary. "Oh, food for thought. I know where to find her." He handed Babe his phone, and there was a short video of Trinity behind the bar at Louie's. "Which means so do other people."

Babe's heart pounded, racing with anger, but he remained calm. "And this is your idea of meeting again as fucking friends? Is this a warning or threat? From our conversation, I thought all was good. I kept my word and managed to keep you in one piece. Had I not seen the car bomb, although it was simplistic, it was enough to destroy you, Noir, and the vehicle. That's just for starters. So what is the shot of Trinity all about?"

Javier swirled his brandy, passing it beneath his nose. "Such a sweet, woodsy aroma. Ah, neither my associates nor I are responsible for the image. I think it may have been your Commander, but I cannot be certain. Just know, the stakes are high in this game you play." He appeared concerned with authenticity—no dramatics. "Babe, I am not your enemy, quite the contrary. Do you really think it wouldn't have already happened if I wanted you or your girlfriend dead?" The man had a point; nonetheless, he despised the cartel and their sleazy, money-grabbing lack of ethics. While he knew Javier's business was lucrative, it didn't change he was up to his neck in unacceptable business ventures. If Babe knew where the trafficked children were, he'd remove them.

The thought reminded him of the two boys with Ruthie on Chestnut Street. While Babe would always think of it as his grandfather's house, he was warming to the idea he might be able to call it home one day, especially if he married Trinity. Those things were a lifetime away, and right now, he had to get out of Cartagena.

"Get me the fuck out of here," Babe stood, the blistering heat of anger exploded up his throat. "What makes you think it is Deary?" Javier shrugged and said he wasn't sure, but if he were laying odds, The Commander would be his pick. He sat so collected, as though their conversation was about the forecast: rain or no rain? *What the fuck.*

"My jet will be at your disposal, and feel free to take the clothes purchased for you. The phone is mine, but you may have it. I hope you are satisfied; I kept my word to you. It would have been a winning proposition to add you to my business, perhaps another time."

Babe turned and headed down the hall. Javier told Seb to have one of the men take the Marine to the airport. Javier was right behind him and motioned to Seb to proceed. A car was waiting at the door to transport him to the jet.

Javier sat, looking into his glass. His mind was moving like clouds before a storm; frankly, he wasn't used to being turned down and hoped the Marine would have found delight in Carmen's arms, forgetting about his friend in New Orleans. The Marine was the only one he'd offered his beautiful sister-in-law to; she was off-limits in the House of Men. Love was overrated, and one day, Babe might regret being tied to Antoine Noelle's daughter. All in all, the Marine had delivered on his promise and protected him and then some. For not knowing the planned massacre ahead of time, a brilliant idea of Noir's, he more than adapted to the situation and took charge of orchestrating their exit. Javier and Noir were unsure of that one piece of the puzzle. How many men would they lose?

Thanks to the big guy, they lost none, and only one was injured, two counting Babe.

Seb knocked on the office door. "You have a call; it's from America."

"Get a name; I think I know who it is. Tell him I cannot come to the phone at the moment but will call him in the morning." The only thing to do was lie to the Commander, claiming his Marine was still on the compound. "Seb, do not answer any questions about the American." The younger man bit his lip, his eyes blinking rapidly. "What happened, Seb?"

Seb shuffled his feet, looking down, swallowing hard, and having difficulty speaking. Javier asked again what had happened. "He asked about the American, and I told him he was on the way to the airport."

Javier closed his eyes and sighed, "Bring me the phone; I'll speak to the man. You need to call the driver and tell him to turn around now." He threw his glass against the wall, yelling a stream of obscenities. He took a deep breath when Seb returned, calming himself and preparing for a conversation.

"Good evening, Commander. Your Marine worked out well."

"And he's coming back to the States?" His voice sounded surly like a growl.

"No, he is checking out a possible problem with one of my competitors. You know, as soon as I eliminate one, another springs up. The larger businesses try to take mine over, or the smaller ones attempt to mingle into my fold, only to assassinate me six months into the business. It is like the rising and setting of the sun. It's a guarantee."

Grumble, then silence. Grumble again. "So, he's not on his way to the States?"

"No, not yet, anyway. I told you I would keep you in the loop. In fact, Babe has spoken highly of you and is considering re—"

"Re-enlisting?" the man's voice boomed through the phone. "I told him civilian life was not for everyone, but now he knows about our little arrangement, I'd have to decline his application." He cleared his throat. "Keep me apprised. I want to know when he is leaving there and arriving here."

The arrogance of the Commander brushed Javier the wrong way. Who did he think he was to give orders? Maybe he'd pay Noir and Babe to take him down. The old guy needed to be taught not to make demands of him.

He knew there'd be a blow-up when the Marine returned. Maybe Babe would get a charge for being hired to assassinate the man. He said he was planning on doing it anyway. Javier could send a message to anyone else in his inner circle; he was not someone to play around with.

The car flew along the roads; the blur of vegetation and flowers was formless in the darkness of night. The phone rang, the driver answered it, and the next thing he knew, the car was making a sharp U-turn, causing horns to blow and people to scream and yell. *Oh, fuck no*, he thought. Mid U, Babe opened the door and rolled out. He had identification papers, ten thousand dollars, a knife, a gun, ammo, and a day's worth of clothes in his bug-out bag. He planned on changing on the way to New Orleans to be refreshed when he saw Trinity.

He sprinted through the thick foliage, heading in the direction of the airport. Javier undoubtedly would try to interfere and flag his name at the airports. He didn't know the lay of the land, so he sat amidst a grove of trees and looked at a map of Cartagena on his phone. He wondered how far away he needed to be to keep the call undetected. The phone rang. It was Javier; he didn't answer it. Then a text came through: NOT MY DOING. DEARY KNEW OF YOUR RETURN. RESPOND ASAP FOR INSTRUCTION. Babe rubbed his temples. *Fuck you, Javier.* This whole thing was one cluster fuck after another. All he wanted was his life back, and it all boomeranged to Chop. *Fuck Deary, Chop's my first stop.* He texted back; NO CAN DO. I'LL TELL YOU WHEN I'M DONE. IF I CAN GET TO YOUR JET, IS THE OFFER STILL THERE? Silence.

Babe decided to wait for the cover of late night to start his way to the airport if he got the okay from Javier. If he didn't get the ride from Javier, he might have to call Antoine, and then the question begged, did Trinity's dad have a plane at his disposal? So many unanswered questions and a blurry future. His side ached from rolling out of the car and hitting the highway. He had road rash on his arms, and his bullet wound was bleeding again. His mind drifted to the setup at Javier's. Clearly, he was pulling in billions with a B. Had he decided to stay at Casa Garcia, he'd be what Javier called a kept man. What he could tell was the men working for him were paid to play pool, cavort with their girlfriends, and hang around with their children.

Then, his brain dinged to the metal building, and he developed a knot in his gut. Surely he wouldn't keep drugs on the premises, or was it where he did his manufacturing? The tenseness in his soul had nothing to do with the drugs. The real gut punch was more about warehousing kids. While he wanted to return to New Orleans, he had to investigate Casa Garcia. If Javier housed abducted children on his property while everyone else on the property was living a life of leisure, he could not and would not allow that to happen. He had to return to Javier.

HAVE THE DRIVER PICK ME UP. HE'LL KNOW WHERE.

ON THE WAY. Interesting, he thought. Had the rules changed?

MILES TO GO

*M*ichael Jackson's "Billie Jean" echoed through Louie's. Trinity and Finn worked to the song, creating a packed house and bar. The news about their entertaining bartending performances ran rampant through the Quarter. Other bars tried to cash in on the action, but Louie's had established the precedent, and it was paying off handsomely. Finn laughed and jumped up on the bar, performing the moonwalk. Trinity was effervescent as she watched him. Finn jumped to the floor, and they continued their repertoire.

"You got some moves for a white kid from the Irish Channel. Moonwalking, what?" she giggled. Since Babe's phone call, though it was briefer than brief, the spark had returned to her eyes, and her smile was beaming from her soul. Tumbling in the recesses of her mind was how to tell her Marine about the innocent, or was it, kiss. Knowing him as she did, he had never been one to be judgy, and maybe it wouldn't make a bean's worth of difference to him. She knew he was being held captive, but had he found pleasures outside their relationship? Before her, he'd never given a second thought to pay-for-play; it was routine. She felt her stomach plummet, like falling and getting the air knocked out of her body when she was a kid. *Not okay; he better not.* She pushed the ideas from her head, and they finished the night out, topping over a thousand dollars in tips. Finn walked her to the hotel like every night they worked together.

After the abduction commotion, it took a while for Trinity to get the courage to leave her parent's house, return to her apartment, and go back to work, but things were settling in, and she knew her man would be coming home to her.

After a few hours of sleep, her phone rang; it was her father. "Dawlin' pack a suitcase and everything you might need for a week, maybe ten days."

"Why?" she asked, trying to clear the cobwebs from her head.

"Just do it. Your Marine friend told me to tell you and provide protection for you. I told him I would. He's on a delicate mission and said they would use you as leverage, interfering with his job." So far, he'd maintained his cool. His daughter could be a handful and was as hard-headed as they came.

"But, Daddy, I have a dog." She threw at him as a reason not to leave.

"Then pack some dog food and bowls. This is not a debate, Trinity; get it done. Big Paul will be at your place in fifteen minutes, so I advise you to get your stuff together. Don't worry about food for you." He heard the objecting huff but also could tell she'd surrendered. He couldn't help but think the Marine meant something deep to her, or it would have never gone so smoothly.

Trinity lugged out her big suitcase and packed as told for ten days. She included all toiletries, grabbed a couple of rolls of toilet paper and tampons, loaded Gunner's bowls and food into a tote, and added her phone charger and laptop. She leashed the dog about the time Big Paul knocked. She remembered thinking her dad's friend was a giant man until she met her Marine. Babe wasn't the tallest guy she'd met; a bunch of the Pelican's pro basketball team frequented Louie's, but combined with his mass, he topped them all. To her, he was the perfect man and a flawless physical specimen. Granted, he needed to work on the mental game, but they could do it together.

Big Paul picked up Trinity's bags, and she held tight to Gunner. They went through the service entrance and into a black SUV. "Who's car is this? Are we going to Mama and Daddy's?"

He looked at her through the rearview mirror, "Mine and no. What radio station do you want?" He wasn't the friendliest of people, and she got the distinct impression she was a pain in his ass, "Any is fine." The man made it clear he wasn't a chatty person and not to ask questions. She snuggled in the seat next to Gunner and listened to the music. "Gunn, your dad will be home, and life will become normal again; you'll see." Her mind wandered. Was she trying to tell the dog or convince herself?

They jumped on the interstate and headed toward the Causeway. Roaming through her mind was question after question. Where in the hell were they going? Was this mute man going to be with her the entire time? At least he hadn't asked for her phone yet.

The SUV bounced along the bridge as it went over the expansion joints. She could feel her face turning green, and the backseat nausea began to set in. "Big Paul, can you crack the windows? Gunner likes to put his head out, and I'm feeling queasy. Can I come up in the front seat?" He glanced back at her and lowered the windows about three inches, hardly enough for Gunner to put his head out, but at least his nose. The fresh wind on her face quelled the approaching car sickness. Big Paul continued to go straight until they were out in the country. He turned left on a gravel road and went for what seemed another mile, maybe more. A freshly painted white fence surrounded the perimeter of a vast piece of land. Three horses frolicked on one side of an old farmhouse while cattle grazed in a big meadow behind. "We are in the middle of bumfuck Egypt. How long do I have to stay here? Ya know I have a job." She pouted like a spoiled child.

"Hey, little girl, this isn't a picnic in the park for me either. Your dad gave the orders, and he's my boss, so like it or not, I am stuck here until he tells me otherwise. Stop your whiny bitching and put your big girl panties on." He carried her bags into the house. An older woman stepped onto the porch, trying to help. "Auntie Inez, sorry about your company," he directed his eyes to Trinity. "She's spoiled rotten. Your chicken started laying eggs again?"

The raised farmhouse was white wood with dark green shutters, a screen porch across the front, and had a look from pictures she'd seen from the "way back in dem days" when her grandparents were chil'ren, as her

Mama's people would say. The older relatives on her side were from Haiti with darker skin, bigger smiles, and catching accents. Trinity felt like she'd stepped back into some other time.

Gunner took off at full speed toward the horses, which continued to graze. Trinity and Babe had taken him to the dog park a few times where he'd try to play with the other dogs, but this was wide open space meant for hauling butt, and he ran in gleeful excitement. "Honey-call, that dog of yours ever been to the country?"

Trinity looked at the woman like she had three heads. "No, why would he? Look, lady—"

"Auntie Inez, honey-call-it." Her smile turned up like a bow as she corrected the girl.

From rolling her eyes to borderline rude, Trinity looked back at her, "My name is Trinity Noelle."

"Beg your pardon, Miss Smarty Pants. I know who you are, and I'm Inez Noelle Sinclair, your daddy's country aunt. My shit smells like flowers, just like yours. Now get ya stuff into the upstairs room on the left, then meet me in the mudroom off the kitchen." So, this was her great aunt, her grandmother, Mere's sister or half-sister. She seemed too young to be Mere's sister. "See you in the mudroom, and Big Paul, you can head on now. We're safe out here. I got Bessie Smith." She picked up a rifle. "Judd has Billy Wesson, so we have us some Smith & Wesson, not to mention the gang calling themselves cowboys," she snickered. "We got four of them, and all have weapons and can shoot. You head on back to the city." Judd was the man in charge, maybe closer to Inez than the others or just a hired hand like the rest, but there was something different about him. He was more than a boy but yet seemingly young for a man. He was probably her age.

Big Paul had a suitcase in his hand and grinned at her. "Wish I could, but Antoine was specific, his message–don't leave her unattended."

Trinity felt overwhelmed and uncomfortable and didn't know what to make of the place or this woman. Yes, Gunner dug the hell out of it, but she wasn't so sure. How would Finn manage the new bar act alone? He better damn well not include Samantha in it.

"Trinity, give me your phone." Reluctantly, she handed it over. He took the battery out, placed it in his pocket, and handed her another phone. Anger redness began piercing her caramel skin.

"Put the battery back in so I can get a number off my phone, now."

"Can't chance it." He refused.

"Jeezum, it'll take a second. Please." Tears were forming in her eyes.

He was hesitant but put the battery back in her phone. She wrote the new number for Babe, quickly handed the phone back, and Paul disassembled it again. Trinity took her replacement phone and went upstairs.

She began her text: Its me. New phone. Out in BFE on a fucking farm.

Babe waited off the road amidst dense foliage and then saw a car coming; it resembled the vehicle he had fled from. He stepped out, hailed it, and maneuvered inside while it was still moving, albeit slowly; nonetheless, there was no stopping, then it squealed off. His phone buzzed; he read the message and nodded, thinking, *Good, Antoine did as asked.* Babe responded: good.

Trinity's mind pinged around. *Good? No, I miss you, or I love you? How are you? Where precisely in BFE?* It seemed like he didn't care. Maybe he wasn't the one for her if he couldn't be more caring. Perhaps he was used to this clandestine activity, but all she wanted was to be back in New Orleans, doing her thang!

She went downstairs to the mudroom. "I'm here. What now?" Babe had hurt her feelings, and she was pissed. Nobody had given her any decent explanation. She wasn't a child; people needed to confer with her, not treat her like a chess piece to move around at will.

Inez handed her a pair of rubber boots. "You'll need these, honey-call-it. The ground is a bit mucky since the rain." The woman smiled again, trying to be nice to the spoiled brat.

"I'm sorry if I've been rude or persnickety, but I have no idea what's going on, and it seems like everybody is treating me like a child. What is going on? My dad said it was for my safety, and my boyfriend asked him." The woman's eyes softened; she understood. Trinity removed her shoes and stepped into a pair of pink-striped Wellington boots.

"Come on, girl. We'll talk while we grab the eggs. I wish Paul would go back to the city. We have everything covered here, but your daddy wants his baby girl watched at all times. You might have some bad people looking for you. We have to hope your manfriend takes care of business soon." Inez was direct but had a spunky personality, which Trinity could get along with if she allowed herself.

She handed the girl a straw hat and a basket to collect eggs. Trinity assumed Auntie Inez would show her how. *Yuck.*

The car pulled back onto Javier's compound. Babe had to strategize getting a peek inside the warehouse. What if it were abducted children? Javier's crew was substantial. Maybe thirty or forty people, considering two rotations doubling what he'd seen in the house, plus all those outside and who knew how many in a surveillance room. The numbers were against him, no doubt.

Javier waited for him in the office. Babe made his way to him. "I'm glad you changed your mind. The Commander knew you were going to New Orleans, so stay here for a few more days and devise a plan to get to him. I don't know how the military works in the U.S. or how easy it is to get to his office or get to him. My gut says if you ask for a meet, just you and him; others will hide in the wings out of sight. You'll be a dead man. He'll deny your request if you say you want to re-enlist." Babe weighed

Javier's sincerity, and either he was an infallible liar, or he was telling the truth.

First things first was getting a look into the metal building. One thing Babe had was the ability to keep a pan face, so no one had any idea what he was thinking. "I think I might know how to handle it. It'll be dicey, but I will process the strategy. Right now, I need some food and rest. I don't know if you sent Carmen into my room or if she did it on her own, but I would appreciate her staying away from me. I need my wits about me, besides—"

"You have your girl. Deal, no women. Now go eat and rest." In other words, he dismissed him; the discussion was over.

The following morning, Babe did what he could of his routine, and Javier hadn't lied; his gym and equipment were stellar. There wasn't much he could do, but he did what he could. Babe felt like an entertainment act, the one where the performer spun multiple plates on sticks to the audience's amazement. His spinners—abducted kids, eliminating Deary, getting back to Trinity, finding Mays, all while keeping tabs on Ruthie and the boys, oh, and keeping a job, if he still had one. He could always hang a shingle and practice law, *as if,* he thought, *no fuckin' way, not when there are so many perverted creatures roaming the streets.*

After working out as much as possible, it was time for a good run, and what a beautiful setting—the compound. The big guy had to get an okay from security, which Javier allowed. Babe ran through the park-like grounds in front of the house, then went around the sides to the back garden, following the path while maintaining silence. The pathway took him by the houses, and then he pushed it to the warehouse. If there were guards, he didn't see them, but he knew there was a likelihood cameras were catching his every move. The door had a padlock, but if people were inside, they would react to the tinkling sound as he trilled his fingers on the metal sheeting. Nothing. Silence. He moved on and continued his run. When he entered the house after cooling off, Javier greeted him.

"What were you looking for at the greenhouse?"

"To see if there were abducted kids. I didn't realize it was a greenhouse." Point blank, no need to bullshit.

"What makes you think I would have abducted children at my home?" Babe could see the register of genuine curiosity.

There was no other way to explain other than directly; if it meant another bullet, then so be it. "Javier, when I stopped Faraday from loading the helo, he had two boys and a hooker—"

"And a shit ton of money, my money. I don't abduct children for abuse; I provide the service of my helicopters and pilots for other people; I am but a pinpoint in the abduction industry." Javier had an expression like there was nothing wrong with what he did; he was making money and lots of it off the kids, even if it was, as he said, a minuscule amount. *That's a big problem, chief.*

"I don't care if you're the one hosing the kids or providing a service for someone else. Ending the machine is my kind of thing: the extermination of pedophiles; that makes my dick hard to coin your expression. I get my rocks off at the thought of putting someone like you out of business." He couldn't have been blunter.

Javier held his jaw in his hand as though contemplating the issue before him. "I can show you where they keep the children if you want to rescue them. Is that it? Do you realize there are hundreds of thousands of children sold around the world, maybe millions? Even you, Mr. Super Marine, can't save them all. I will gladly show you, but you'll need to figure out how to transport them. Your United States knows about them and doesn't want to deal with it; it's a bit like the Jews in World War II. You don't know the half of it. The greatest power in the world, at least for the time being, and they do nothing. Why? Some important people in your government are paying top dollar for the children; the younger, the better. So you, one man, are going to take on the massive problem? I think not."

The thought of hundreds of thousands of children was overwhelming, let alone a million. "Faraday was flying your helo and bringing kids to you, no?" He looked him square in the eyes. "What if it were one of the children swimming in your pool? What then?" The look on Javier's face created angst in Babe. It wasn't fear of being hurt or killed; that was bound to come in due time. Babe's muscles flexed with tension; he felt his blood racing through his body and his heart pounding in his chest, almost deafening in his ears. There wasn't a solution; it was the way of the world. Was he supposed to be okay with it? No, he wanted to kill each and every piece of shit molester and person or persons involved in the whole fucking business. "I wanted to make a point by mentioning the kids in your pool, not to offend or insinuate anything. But let me be clear; I will kill anyone I see take a child, hurt a child, or hose one. Been there, done that, and will fucking do it again." Babe was letting his primal self rear its head. His body quivered with madness.

"One of my men will take you and show you. Then, Marine, do as you please. A thought for you. Who created this burning inside you to be the hero of the children? Were you one of those kids?" Javier stuck his hands in his pockets with a smug look on his face, like he was spotlighting some massive revelation.

"Are you fucking kidding me? Yeah, I was an abused kid until I took care of business at twelve years old. Maybe not taking it up the ass but getting the crap beat out of me. Fucking right and every degenerate on the street reminds me of Gino Vicarelli, and I kill them whenever I can. It's like swatting fucking flies; some get away, sometimes, but I'll wait for another opportunity and strike." His face reddened with the uptick in his heart rate, and his posture became more rigid.

Javier poured a glass of whiskey, offering one to Babe, who was so incensed he didn't notice. "Ah," Javier nodded. "So that's what rages the heat in you. Is it why you don't have any qualms about taking a life, making you, in your mind, some bad motherfucker?" He raised his eyebrows and shifted like a boxer in the ring, heightening the sarcasm. "You don't get it. Nobody wants these children, nobody! I should drop you right now, but I hear your concern and desire to make things better. I know it to be sincere. Plain and simple, you can't stop it. Save what you can today because you are flying back to the States tonight with kids or not. Pick a different cause because that's a losing proposition."

Babe clenched his fists; he wanted to hurt someone, to kill someone, because he knew Javier was right. He felt his breathing begin to rage like a wild animal. His vision changed as his pupils blew out. There was no way he could do it by himself, and he felt at a loss. "You've given me things to think about, and I will; you have my word. Well, I have one for you. Couldn't you turn it around and do away with the people buying the kids from you?"

Javier shook his head and turned away, walking to the office. "Get your head out of your ass. Perversity, as you see it, has been going on since the beginning of time—"

Babe bellowed, "But it doesn't make it right or even a little okay. Javier, you have to see that." He flung his arms in front of him, displaying a mania side Javier hadn't seen. The controlled Marine was losing his shit.

The bossman raised his hands and softly spoke, easing the atmosphere. "You sound like my friend, Mateo, the one murdered by, I believe, his sister. He was against the business of sex trafficking." He paced back and forth behind his desk, pointing at Babe. "I told him he was losing billions of dollars. Billions, Marine, but no, he was dead against it like you. Maybe it got him assassinated because he opposed the new business practices." Javier was animated. "Fuck, he didn't charge your Commander Deary to get those Marines safely back to the U.S. Mateo was strong and a good businessman, do not misunderstand, but he wasn't willing to change. Maybe it was a blessing he sent me off instead of someone else the day of the explosion. It made it so I could take the business and build it." He became lost in his rambling. Both stoic, silent men appeared to let all their pent-up emotions loose, neither winning the battle nor giving in, breaking their controlled silence. It was a lose-lose. "Like I said before, know your enemy, and I, believe it or not, am not your enemy. As you respect me, not out of fear, so I respect you. It is time to part ways for the time being."

PRIORITIES

*O*nce in the car and on his way again, the driver turned in the opposite direction from the airport. The driver, who spoke very little English, attempted to explain. "We go to get for you. One, two, three?" He turned his hand up in question.

Javier was holding to his word, and the driver was taking him to see or get the children. *Okay,* he thought, *what do I do with them when I get to New Orleans? They don't know the language. Maybe if I get the location, I'll know or find out who to report it to; oh shit. What the fuck is wrong with me? Sex trafficking is not my fight, but is it? I am hardly prepared for this. Fucking Chop. It all started with him.* "How much money for one?" The driver watched him in the rearview mirror but didn't respond. "Dinero? Uno?"

"American dollar?" the driver asked.

"Si." So far, he barely communicated but made himself understood.

"Ten t'ousand. I get for you." He did not doubt the driver's word, but like most places when dealing in illegal pursuits, everyone always got their cut. He speculated it was nine thousand, and the driver was pocketing a thousand for himself. The rest of the ride was quiet as thoughts mulled through his mind.

It seemed only yesterday he was alongside the team fighting in hot pursuit of insane extremists or standing before Commander Deary, discussing separation from the Corps. Here, he was mixed up in some nightmare that had become his reality. All he wanted was a steady, comfortable life and maybe, possibly, to vacate the demons in him; the battle was against the demons and what he needed to fight. His propensity for taking everyday street thugs out paled in proportion to this global perversity. He was only one man looking for normalcy, and it seemed every time he turned around, there was another monster and not one he conjured or contrived because of guilt.

Afghanistan, Africa, Iraq, and Argentina were over and done for him, yet here he was in Colombia. He couldn't handle the enormity of threats; perhaps it best to end it all—one well-placed bullet would stop the demons, end his obsessive need to right wrongs, and free Trinity to find a partner for life without the non-stop burden. The misery he had experienced in one lifetime was more than he could bear. The bad guys were winning. *Fucking Chop.* This new awareness compounded his ever-present array of disorders. He didn't want the revelation about trafficking kids; he could do nothing but maybe check out.

The car turned onto a rustic gravel road with potholes the size of craters jostling him from side to side, pulling on his puncture. They pulled up to a makeshift metal building built with scraps of varying dimensions. Hidden amongst thick foliage and overgrowth, it was barely visible. The place would have gone unnoticed if he hadn't been looking for it. The nameless driver stopped the vehicle, put his hand out, telling Babe to stay, and asked for the money, which he immediately pulled from his bug-out bag.

Three minutes later, he returned with a boy probably twelve years of age. The odd thing was Babe recognized him, and the widening of the boy's eyes expressed the same. Babe touched his lips, indicating the boy to stay quiet. *Un-fucking believable.* Of all the abducted kids, it ended up being one of the street kids always hanging around the French Market. Babe felt sure the kid knew Chris and Reg.

The driver turned the car around and sent gravel and mud flying as he spun out onto the main road, hauling ass to the airport. The boy kept looking at Babe, he guessed, trying to size up the situation. What did this man want from him? When they drove onto the tarmac, the jet was ready for boarding—no documents were required. He'd call Antoine to arrange a lift once he arrived in New Orleans. "Thanks for the ride," he commented to the driver. The whole episode made him sick, like he could vomit right then and there. And the fucking blister that rubbed on his soul, to hell with the proverbial icing on the cake, everyone was in on the action—the high and mighty, *fuck 'em all.*

Once onboard, the boy sat back with a sullen, downturned appearance. "Kid, what's your name? I'm Babe." The big man did his best at a warm smile, but such was not his nature at the time, or ever, he contemplated, unless he was with Trinity. Everything was better with his woman if she still wanted him. "Chris and Reg live at my house. I think you know them." He attempted to lighten the atmosphere, maybe invoking some calm in the boy.

"Jacob," he said with a look of surprise. "You already have boys. What do you want with me?" *Ah, so he thinks I'm a perve*; Babe started to understand and quickly allayed any of his fears. He asked why the boy was on the street. The answer was surprising. Jacob was the son of a prostitute who overdosed and died, thus leaving him orphaned. He wasn't in the system anywhere. One of his mom's friends taught him to read and write, but the kids on the street taught him about numbers, life, and money. "I ain't no whore, mister."

"I should hope not," Babe responded with an authoritative voice. "You hungry? I am." He stood and checked the secured cabinets and found an assortment of snacks and drinks. He handed Jacob a bag of chips, an apple, and a Coke. Babe tucked into an apple, Chex mix, and water. He felt like he could use a guzzle of scotch but refrained. He was mentally and physically exhausted. The pit in his stomach, while getting filled with food, remained void, creating a sinking feeling throughout his body; maybe the fatigue was more mental and emotional, *fuck you, doc, I do feel.* "You tired, kid, or need the men's room? If so, it's right here," putting his hand on a door. "I have a few calls, but then I'm getting some shut-eye; why don't you try."

The boy reclined as much as he could and turned on his side away from the big man. He called Javier to find out where he would be landing. Their conversation was like old friends, but the thing was, Babe didn't have friends; he trusted very few since he was a kid, maybe the age of the boy.

Next in line was Antoine. He called. "Antoine Noelle." The man answered.

"Sir, this is Babe Vica—"

Antoine interrupted, "I know your voice, Marine. Where does everything stand?"

"Flying into Lakefront. Private. I need a lift and want to stay under the radar."

"Done. Time?"

"I'll text when we start the descent. Oh, and I have an extra passenger."

Being in the country was not Trinity's idea of amusement. The more she thought about things, the more she realized being with Babe had brought on all kinds of oddities, not to mention danger. It felt like she was living in a damn soap opera and had to figure out priorities; suddenly, she realized she wasn't living her best life, and something would have to change. He had crazy fucking contacts, scary hallucinations out of the blue, couldn't watch the news, didn't want to dance, and frankly, Babe killed people; he'd said so himself. What kind of man would Babe be as a lifelong partner? Now, she was stuck in BFE because he sent orders, and she was in danger again! *Orders? Oh, but no!*

Maybe this break from everything helped her to see things with a clearer head. Upon reflection, she traced back some of the other elements of their relationship. Okay, so she was the first girl he'd ever loved. He was insanely loyal, badass to the bone, and then there was his body and intense stare like he was looking into her soul. *Badass but sweet, hm,* the thought rumbled through her mind: *he would die for me, period.* Whatever he did was for her protection or well-being. Those facts were hard-core truths. The most important and meaningful factor was she was in love with him, a love like never before. It wasn't the infatuation of acting grown and married as it had been with Joey. Things with Babe were as real as they got.

Trinity walked through the pasture; the cows barely turned their heads. She approached one with caution. They were sizeable beasts and could run her over like a freight train, but they had such sweet eyes. Like a frustrated driver blowing their horn, the thought shockingly blew into her brain— Babe's eyes captured her, and his intensity was hot. The internal debate about the pros and cons of being Babe's partner rolled through like a slow-moving fog bank on the Mississippi when the weather changed.

A voice carried through the pasture, "Girl, don't you go off too far. I need some help over here." She couldn't deny Auntie Inez. The woman could go on and on about nothing or impart some straight-up wisdom. She needn't worry; Big Paul was maybe a hundred yards from her, and the farmhands were forever gawking and would spy anything out of the ordinary, especially Judd. She had seen how he watched her and wasn't sure she got a good feeling from the observation. Judd was handsome in a country way—shaggy hair, scruff beard, and a piece of hay or something hanging from his mouth as he twirled it with his tongue. The western hat, cowboy boots, and Wrangler jeans added to the look. His body seemed taut, what she could tell from the way his shirt hugged his body, but something grabbed her attention. Was it desire? Curiosity? The thought was sheer angst from all the uncertainties in her life.

Through a choke of brewing tears, she whispered, "Babe, come back to me."

Jacob dozed, checking Babe from time to time. The boy waited for the other shoe to drop. The big guy looked frightening but had acted nice, just quiet. His life had been scary, starting with the abduction by two men with masks, then waking up after being drugged in an old uncomfortable plane; destination unknown, purpose unknown, but definitely casting a bleak shadow on his future. This stranger cat-napped throughout the flight back to New Orleans.

Babe would bring the boy to Chestnut St.; then he'd be off to Quantico or wherever Deary was based. The question now was how to find out where Deary was; who did he know who could access the information? Then it twigged; Daniel Collins worked at the complex in Algiers, close to New Orleans.

Commander Deary had taken a keen interest in Babe from the first time they met and was a person the Marine held in high regard. *Colossal mistake, in hindsight.* His suspicion of the man was triggered because he seemed to want to get too close, but he had sluffed it off, just like when Chop showed up at Louie's. The Commander had sought him out for a need-to-know assignment involving killing Yuhn, a fellow Marine. Something stunk then, but the Commander saught him out, so it had to be on the up and up, right? *Wrong.*

He had to find the turn-coat of the highest degree, the Commander. Deary could've been at Quantico, or did he finally get moved to his hometown in Algiers, across the river from New Orleans?

The jet landed, and on the tarmac was a car waiting for them. The headlights blinked twice, which meant he was almost home, and the emptiness in his gut would be filled with his woman. Some of the excited feelings he experienced were new and hard to define. It wasn't the rapid heart rate, tweaked senses, and kinetic energy his body felt heading on an assignment. The emotion was far more profound in his body, maybe something to do with his soul. Babe headed for the vehicle with Jacob at his side. The little guy skippy-jogged, trying to keep up with the adult's long strides and fast pace.

The driver got out of the car as they approached. Natural instinct called for Babe to step in front of the kid, blocking him from the man standing next to the vehicle. Standing ready to serve, he nodded at Babe and the boy as he opened the door for them. Within a minute, they were heading out of the Lakefront airport. "Where to?"

Babe rattled off the street where he had parked his truck, which may or may not have been booted, ticketed, or towed. His mind flashed back to the abduction and how it transpired. Everything pointed straight at his poor decisions to ignore red flags or intense reactions in his gut. He knew someone had been in the apartment. Before allowing Trinity further, he should have scoured the place to determine if there was an intruder or what was the something different. It could have just as easily been a bomb. *Dammit!* Then thought sprung forth like a jack-in-the-box; snake, rent, bills, work, he'd been gone a long-ass time. They pulled up to his truck. *No boot, someone was smiling down at him, maybe his grandfather.*

First things first, he needed to drop the boy at Chestnut and then check on the status of his apartment, or was it still his? Driving to Chestnut, he called Antoine, who immediately answered, "Antoine Noelle." He knew it was early, being six in the morning, but he had to call.

"Sir, thanks for the ride. I've got to take care of some things; I've been gone a long time. Once I ensure any loose ends are neutralized, I'll call Trinity."

There were a thousand things he'd like to say to her father. He felt guilty because he'd put Trinity in danger, which topped his list, as well as the heartburn he'd probably caused the man by having to move her to a safe house.

Trinity's dad cleared his throat, "We paid your rent and bills and had all the tickets removed from your vehicle. You have a sizeable truck, but then you're a big fella. As soon as you've created a safe situation, let me know. I'm sure she's being a pain in my aunt's ass. I've indulged her too much. Good to have you back, Marine."

"Thank you, sir. I'll be in touch." Was he now indebted to Mr. Noelle?

The drive to Chestnut took twenty minutes, and the boy was like a non-stop stream of questions. He understood the boy's trepidation. He pulled into the driveway, and they entered the house. Still in her robe, Ruthie ran up to him with a heart-filled smile and tears glossing her eyes. "Boy, you've had me in a state. Where have you been?" Her questions came across in a scolding manner laced with care.

"Long story and one for another time." She nodded. "This is Jacob; can you get him settled? I still have a few things to tidy up." Reg and Chris sounded like a herd of animals running down the stairs. Ruthie cleared her throat loudly, and the running ceased immediately. Both boys lit up when they saw him; then they spotted Jacob.

"Dude," Chris told the younger boy, "We thought you were toast. You like disappeared; we all thought you'd gotten—" They stopped, realizing it hadn't been long since they had had their misfortune. Chris asked Babe, "Is he staying here, too?" The big guy nodded. "Ma'am, can we take him upstairs so he can change or something? And what about school?"

Ruthie pinned her shoulders back with a stance; she was undoubtedly in charge. "If you mean a shower, the sooner, the better. The boy smells dirty. Let him wear your pajamas even if they are too big," she said to Reg, the smaller of the two boys. "We'll get him fixed up later today. First, Jacob, do you need to eat right away? I'm starting breakfast now. How do you take your eggs?" He told her no, and the three scampered up the stairs. "Chris and Reg, best you come right back down after you settle the boy."

"I have to run by my place to get my phone and some things, but I'll be back." She rolled her eyes with a hand on her hip, saying she'd heard that before, but for him to be on his way. "Ruthie, it's a story between us for another time." He winked.

"Go 'head with ya'self." He felt sure the old gal had things in order. She'd even made him feel a bit dressed down, which gave him an inward chuckle. He could have used a Ruthie when he was a kid. She'd have kicked Gino Vicarelli's ass.

Conveniently, he found a parking spot close to the apartment. His mind was on a million different things, but he needed to set his awareness on his immediate surroundings. Out of the corner of his eye, he saw a group of punk teenagers keeping pace on the other side of the street. *Not today,* he thought. *There's too much shit already, and it's only seven. Yep,* he watched two peal off and crossed behind maybe twenty feet. Babe raised his voice, "Don't pick a fight you can't win. I advise you to head off on your merry way, motherfuckers." He stopped and turned to face the two. Seeing the intimidating glare and perceived demonic appearance from the massive man, they crossed back and joined their group, turning at the next block.

Thankfully, the apartment was like it had been before—nothing untoward pierced the atmosphere. Babe's phone was lying plugged in on his desk. Immediately, he called NOPD and explained the situation. Dispatch said they'd have officers on the lookout.

Once the call ended, he looked through his contacts and found Daniel's number. He'd been a good combat Marine, dedicated to the Corps. An unfortunate run-in with an IED took his left leg; he'd been lucky. The other two Marines were not as fortunate and paid the ultimate price. Babe closed his eyes; feelings of guilt washed over his body like the breaking waves on a beachfront. The sickening twist in the gut always followed, and the same question rolled like marbles through his head: *Why not me?* The sentiment followed him like a curse.

Sitting in the desk chair, he leaned forward, rubbing his head. There would never be an answer to the question. He shook it off and called Daniel, hoping he'd pick up. "Collins."

"Collins, this is Vicarelli." Silence for a moment. He wondered if the Marine remembered their last time together. Babe had held Collins' mutilated body, moving him to safety and a medic, who called it in, and the last he saw was Collins on the winch stretcher as it hoisted through the air and into a rescue copter.

"Yes, sir," Collins cleared his throat. "How are you, Captain? I heard you are free and clear, right? Where you livin'?"

"Affirmative, and back in NOLA." Babe hated small talk, but he couldn't blurt out "Where is Deary?" without raising a flag. "Maybe we can grab a beer sometime. I've spoken to Hurley, who told me you were in Algiers. They good to you there?"

"Yes, sir. I like it. I owe you my life, sir. I've often wondered if our paths would cross again so I could tell you thanks. No BS; I mean it. Now, what can I do for you?" Babe could hear a liveliness in the Marine's voice.

"Do you know if Commander Deary is still at Quantico or Norfolk?" He hoped he sounded reasonable enough not to set off any alarms. He leaned on the desk, holding the phone to his ear, equipped with a pad and pen in case there was some pertinent information.

"No, sir. He is here in Algiers, down the hall from me. He's not here yet, but I can give him a message to call you."

"Thanks, but no, I want to come unannounced. Deary and I were pretty close; in fact, he questioned me about my decision to separate from the Corps. This call is between you and me, Collins." He thought the conversation went along controlled and benign. Babe already knew the house where the Commander lived in Algiers; it had been a family home for generations, so he was told a hundred-plus times. Norfolk would have been more challenging, maybe impossible. *Nothing is impossible. That's another lie.*

"He knocks off at seventeen hundred but is here most of the time from zero-eight hundred until—"

"Good to know, Collins, good to know." He needed to wind up the call. He didn't want any reminiscing or idle chatter. "Well, I don't want to keep you from your duties. It was good to hear your voice, and maybe we can grab a drink sometime." Babe's mind was already reeling in the hot pursuit of justice. The Commander was dirty and needed to be put down like any other treasonous bastard. Babe could pull off a look of shock when the message came out that the Commander was dead since he barely showed emotion anyway. He would have to plan this execution to perfection without any evidence left behind.

After the call with Collins ended, Babe investigated recent murders in Algiers, hoping to mimic the crimes. Using the phone provided by Javier, the police couldn't trace it to him; besides, it would have long since disappeared into the river as a smattering of pieces. He had much to plan.

TOO MUCH
COUNTRY

"Trinity-bae, you ever gonna get out of bed? Too much lyin' in the bed isn't good for your lungs; besides, I need your help hanging the sheets." *Hanging the sheets?* It was another of Inez's attempts to lure her downstairs. She rolled over, slid her feet to the floor, and slowly descended into the great room, still donned in a silk head wrap. "Look, I have some eggs still warm and some toast-bread. Girl, you need to eat." Inez meddled in the kitchen, making herself seem occupied.

"No, ma'am, what I need is to get back to the city and my job. Being here is doing nothing good for anyone." Big Paul was sitting on the sofa reading the paper and ignoring the girl. "See, even Big Paul wants to get back to the city." She plated the eggs and toast and sat on the coffee table before the man. "Are you married, Big Paul? If so, what does your wife think of this arrangement?" He looked up from the paper with a slight hint of a smile hidden deep in his eyes. "I see a glimmer; you wanna get out of here as much as I do."

He folded the paper, set it next to him, and looked at her eye to eye. "Trinity, you are a pain in my ass." Paul's phone buzzed. "Where? Did you stop them? How many? Send Judd." He told Trinity to go back upstairs and take her food with her. Glances jockeyed around the room. Judd burst into the mudroom door, shotgun in hand. Paul snapped his fingers and pointed upstairs. Both Inez and Trinity went up the stairs. Walking to Trinity's room, Inez opened an invisible door in the hall, shushed the girl, and brought her inside, closing the door behind them.

Trinity could hear muffled yelling between the stable hands and other male voices. Judd's voice rang out. "Mister, I think you turned down the wrong road." She heard Gunner's ferocious growl.

"Boy, you better keep your hound controlled. I'm here for a girl."

"We don't got a girl here. I wish we did, but you need to find a girl somewhere else. Not on my property." She heard as the voices escalated. "The only girl we had here is long gone to New Orleans. If you came from there, you wasted a trip. This here is private property; if you don't get off my land, I'll take care of business." She and Inez heard two booming gunshots echo from outside. Talking to one of the farmhands, he asked, "You call the sheriff?" Trinity heard a couple of vehicles speeding along the rocky road. "I told ya; get your sorry asses off my property, or else the deputies will take you into custody, and they don't call it St. Slammany for nothing. You fuck with the wrong people in these parts, and you're gone. You stay gone, you hear me?"

Trinity listened. While Judd seemed boyish in many ways, the blond-haired, blue-eyed white boy took to leadership like a duck to water. He was so much more than just a farmhand.

Inez leaned against the door. "See, child, I told you to mind ya'self. I suspect they'll come back tonight with reinforcements. I'm calling ya daddy because it's gonna get nasty here and soon. He may want you back in the city." She unlatched the door, and they left the safe room. "Pack all ya stuff, in case."

The voices trailed up the stairs. Big Paul was on the phone with her father. Judd was talking with one of the hands. The plan was if Antoine wanted Princess home, Paul would take one of the pick-ups. They'd have three trucks all heading in different directions, so it would be a crap shoot as to which one the city boys picked to tail. Commotion brewed, and tensions escalated. Trinity packed her things and waited for instructions. Babe had been right; they would get to him through her.

Babe quickly skirted streets and alleys and hailed a cab to Chestnut Street again. He went in through the back. Ruthie had a pot of gumbo simmering on the stove and was startled when he entered. Her whole body twitched, and she grabbed her chest. "Didn't mean to scare you, ma'am. Smells good. Boys causing any trouble?" She shook her head, spooned a small helping of the gumbo into a bowl, and handed it to him. "Rice isn't ready yet, but the gumbo's good for a taste. Wait another twenty minutes for the rice and bread. Do you like potato salad in your gumbo or on the side?" Even though she'd said it wasn't quite ready, it tasted good.

"On the side, but don't trouble yourself on my account." His phone buzzed.

Antoine said there'd been an incident in the country; hence, Big Paul might bring her to the city. How anyone could have known about Trinity being in Folsom was puzzling and disturbing. They had a safe room for her, but Antoine didn't put it past them to set the house on fire so his baby girl couldn't stay. Babe could feel the back of his neck redden as the anger crested in his gut. He wanted to wait at least a day before doing anything to the Commander in case the police tried to link the disappearance to him since the recent phone call to Daniel. After investigating the killings, he found three of the latest murders, carjackings in Terrytown. It'd be like shooting fish in a barrel.

"Marine, tell me who, and I'll get it done. Give me addresses." Part of him wanted to do the deed for satisfaction, but another part said it would be good to have someone from Antoine's deck handle it. Was pride getting in his way? What had the priest at St. Dominic's said? Pride comes before the Fall. Was he being prideful or stubborn? The thought ticked over in his mind.

"Hang tight, sir; I'll get back to you, but like I said before, I have to do it." *But why?* He wouldn't do it on the Support Facility campus. If he did it outside the Commander's house when he got home, there were too many Ring doorbell cameras. No, he'd go to his office after he'd taken out the people in Folsom. Babe called Antoine, "How do I get to the house in Folsom?" The instructions were straightforward, and her dad wanted to know what the plans entailed. It would be fundamental, boot-basic kinda stuff—eliminate the threat in Folsom.

The relationship with Javier was one of mutual respect, even if he was cartel. The man had kept his word, which gave him cred in Babe's eyes. He hadn't shown any allegiance to the Commander; if anything, he used him to get what he needed, nothing more. If he had been on the same side as the Commander, he would have given him info on Babe, thus a call to Javier. "Hello and Buenos dias. I get that right?" Javier chuckled. "How certain are you, Deary wants me dead?" Response: One hundred percent.

"What is your hesitation, Marine? He's coming for you even if it means taking out your lady friend to get to you. Live or die; you or him. What do they say? It's a no-brainer." Whether it was from having it drilled into him, Marines were loyal to the Corps, period. Was loyalty the issue? *The thing of it*, he thought, *the Commander had put the code of the Corps to the wayside for personal gain.* Like Chop, he'd given up his right to claim to be a Marine. Dilemma solved.

"I'm a Marine; he was a Marine; it's a code we live by, and he broke it. Fuck, he was one of the people manic about our purpose. So, to answer you, there is no hesitation."

On more than one occasion, Javier had mentioned too much seed in a man's body made the resolve weak. *Perhaps, but it sounded so Latin machismo.* Getting laid was not his top priority at the moment; he'd have Trinity all in due time.

Top of the agenda was getting to Folsom. The Mercedes didn't have the power his two-fifty had; given the circumstances, he'd park the sedan and take the truck.

Antoine called Paul with the instruction not to move Trinity. Babe was on the way, and together they would control the situation. He asked if any of the farm hands were new. Inez's place had always been safe and secure; there had to be an infiltrator amidst the group.

Trinity returned to the bed, covers close to covering her head. Her phone vibrated. "Yeah?" When she heard Babe's voice, she sat upright. "Where are you?" He answered on his way to her.

The th-thump of the expansion joints on the bridge was hypnotic and thrust him to the first drive to Pensacola with the debacle of Chop's junkie wife. If he had told Chop to fuck off, none of this shit would be happening. The past months would have been ordinary days. Work out, run with Gunner to the job, run back home, shower, and then Louie's to see his sexy lady and grab a bite. Chop had come to track Trinity, place eyes on her, and figure out if she was worth the hassle. The answer was crystal clear. Yes, she was beautiful and emanated sensuality, but he didn't know she was Antoine Noelle's daughter, just like he hadn't known she was his woman. Trinity was a significant distraction and had taken Babe off his game. He'd lost an edge for a hot minute but was back in full stride, and he'd be unstoppable.

After an hour and ten minutes, he turned onto the gravel road, creating a wake of dust behind him. As he pulled up, Judd stepped out of the house and headed toward the two-fifty. The expression on the young guy's face was like so many others when they saw him for the first time. Babe was an impressive specimen, and anyone could tell he was past done and all out of give a fucks. There'd be no game-playing; it was no-nonsense and as badass as it got. Barking orders, he told Judd he wanted all the farm hands ASAP. They needed to bring their guns or any weapons they had. He would spell out the instructions with no room for personal interpretation, machismo, or hero-nonsense.

Trinity bubbled like a little girl in anticipation as he entered the door. She jumped into his arms. He kissed her briefly and held her for a quick second. "More later, but right now, make yourself scarce. It's about to get real." Part of the orders entailed all farmhands to come to the rear of the house, "Paul, it's up to you if you want to be there or not. I know where your allegiance lies. These motherfuckers," talking about the farmhands, "I don't know 'em from Adam. I don't want Trinity anywhere around to witness this."

Inez came from the kitchen with a big glass of iced tea. "I suppose you'd be Trinity's boyfriend. Mister, you are some kinda big. Now, she says you're sweet, but you don't look too sweet to me, no sir." She handed him the glass and had the other hand on her hip.

Babe breathed heavily like a penned bull, intending to throw anyone to the ground that got in his way. "Ma'am, if we could have a word in private?" She led him into the mudroom and closed the door. "Who's Judd to you? I know he's not some kid you felt sorry for."

The older woman tilted her head. "I'll tell you because of all the crap going on, but it is not common knowledge, you hear me?" Babe nodded, eyes squinted, intensely watching Inez. "Judd's my son. After my husband passed, I was still a young woman in my early forties. I went to town, meaning Covington, to make groceries. There was this fine-looking white—"

Babe interrupted. "I needed to know who he was, not your intimate business. Is the boy trustworthy and dependable?"

"Yes, indeed. Judd doesn't know I'm his momma." Her eyebrows drew together, forming a vertical line between the brows.

"You know the other boys?" He looked down at her, trying not to be intimidating; the gal seemed shaken by his presence.

"Uh, mostly. The ginger-headed boy is new to the area. I found him scrounging for work at the Home Depot, but no one would take him because of his age, I suppose." She scratched her head. The question then became how did anyone know Trinity's location. If these were average teens working the farm for cash in their pockets, then none of them had compromised the safe house.

Babe thanked her for the information and went outside to Paul's vehicle. After thoroughly sweeping the car, he found an air tag tucked in behind the side view mirror and returned to the house. "Paul, they tagged you." He dangled the simple tag in the air. "You can get 'em off Amazon; they're easy to hide. Cartel's not after Trinity; this is the crafty, dishonest dealings of Commander Deary. His men are probably rogue Marines, well-trained, just didn't pass muster or decided to take their training to the private sector. It's not gonna be pretty, but we got this."

Deary knew Trinity was a Noelle and probably tagged all the vehicles on the first floor of the hotel parking garage. The Commander would get his comeuppance for sure. It was all a matter of time.

Babe stripped to his tee shirt and jeans, hanging his denim shirt on the newel post at the bottom of the staircase. He called Judd inside and asked him to make a rough map of the property. Twin oak trees stood about three hundred feet from the start of their gravel road, giving a vantage point to take out the driver and shotgun passenger from the first vehicle. He'd dot the property with a couple of other boys, but he had to have his sharpest shooter in one of the towering oaks; according to the lady of the house, Judd was as close to a sharpshooter as anyone in the trained forces. Inez would be in the safe room with Trinity; Paul would stand guard outside the room, and Babe would sniper from the roof, picking the ones off that got through the boys. The ginger-haired boy would handle the mudroom door. If it came to it, he would jump off the porch roof and meet the intruders in the yard.

Inez called the Sheriff and told him not to be surprised when he received calls about her property resembling a shootout from some gang-related cop show. The good people of Folsom loved their churches, schools, and the Second Amendment and took protecting their own to heart.

As figured, Sheriff Hardy suggested some of his deputies wait at her house and try to handle the altercation without violence. Inez appreciated the gesture, and if it was what the Sheriff wanted to attempt, she was all for it but worried a couple of his men might get shot. "These are bad people, Larry. We like you as Sheriff because you look the other way and let us handle things for ourselves. I wouldn't say no to a couple of your people joining my farm hands, but we won't be following the letter of the law per se; at least, not your law. It's your call, hon. By the way, how's your momma and daddy? Tell them I said hey and asked after them; oh, and sugar plum, we got too many yard eggs if y'all want some." Babe grinned, one side of his mouth broader than the other. *Small country towns, gotta love 'em.*

"You have anything stronger than iced tea here?" She pulled a bottle of Jack Daniels out of her pantry and handed him a glass. "Jack? I guess any port in the storm."

He sipped the bourbon while he contemplated the what-ifs of the conflict du jour. Life had gotten out of control, and once again, he reflected on Chop and then chastised himself for opening the box. Once the evening's conflict was over, they'd return to the city, and Deary would be front and center of his thoughts. Eventually, he'd get to Chop with Javier's blessings.

Disappointment was a feeling he'd never experienced before because he didn't have expectations of anyone. He didn't let people get close; there hadn't ever been a need. It was the perfect term when he thought about the man, though. He had respected Deary and held him in high esteem. Babe understood his superior did what he had to when he accepted the help of a cartel if it was an accurate account. It was the only way to get his people out of a disadvantaged, lose-lose situation where their lives were on the line. The Mateo Moreno person did him a solid, so he felt he owed the favor; he was totally cool with that, even if it sounded like horseshit. Why would Deary hold resentment toward Babe and want him dead? Did the Commander climb in bed with Javier in the trafficking business? Is that what the problem was? Why would he do it? It wouldn't have gone any farther, but the Commander opened the box, threatening him and Trinity—a question he planned on asking when he had Deary's undivided attention.

A thought ran through his mind. What if it was the cartel? With all the drama seeming to envelop him, Babe had difficulty exacting fact from fiction. Who was the good guy or bad guy, or were they all bad? Why would he have let him go and provided the transportation if he had wanted him? Javier wouldn't be so inclined. Nothing made sense. No doubt, if the man wanted him dead, he'd already be six feet under or food for the fish.

If he were a betting person, he'd take odds the people coming for Trinity would strike with the veil of night. Babe called Judd over, "You boys hunt?" He asked, surmising the answer, "I suspect you do, being from these parts. Do y'all ever use night vision goggles?" The boy tried to skirt the issue, saying yes, they all had them but never used them to hunt, just to make sure they didn't shoot each other by mistake. "I don't care if you use them or not. They'll come in handy tonight. I'm fairly certain the men coming here later will have them. Your only advantage is you know the property."

There would be a couple of hours' reprieve. Babe grabbed his shirt off the post and headed up the stairs. He lightly tapped on what he assumed was Trinity's room. She was in bed under the covers. "You took long enough. Come here, my man. It's about to get real!" She quoted him with a throaty laugh. "I've missed you. Now get them clothes off, boy."

Babe stripped in a hot second and got under the covers with her. "Thinking of you got me through some long nights."

Commander Deary paced in his office, waiting for a call from the group of five he'd sent to retrieve Trinity. It was the one surefire way to flush the Marine out. While he felt a touch of regret taking his man out, there wasn't any other choice. He knew the only reason Babe agreed to Javier's proposition was all about obeying his superior's nod of approval. The whole situation was fucked up. Deary had too many secrets and had set a steady slide down the slope.

Years before, a Mexican drug operation involving ruthless people trapped some of his men amid their mission to obliterate and bring to justice those involved, but it backfired. His only answer was to accept the help of Mateo Moreno. Even though he was in Colombia, his influence was like tentacles stretching far, and now the Commander was indebted to his organization and the new capo Javier Garcia. Mateo had never called upon Deary and probably wouldn't have, but Javier Garcia was the new generation of the cartel with exploits not only of drug manufacturing and distribution but also working with the Chinese, adding to the fentanyl problem facing the U.S.

The biggest money maker was human trafficking. Even though he didn't orchestrate the daily buy and sell, he did provide transportation while he moved his drugs. Javier could make a handsome sum by providing a means for those with the inclination to sell labor and sex exploits, which earned billions of dollars more than the airline businesses or expansive conglomerations. For Javier, it was all about making money; the how didn't matter. He reaped aplenty without being directly involved, a piece of the pie, so to speak.

The chain started with Javier's helicopters; they brought the drugs and abducted the children from hot spots in the United States. Then, the children were delivered to a base in Colombia and dispersed to the highest bidders, usually through brokers from the rich and famous— mostly Americans. The complex arrangement gave the buyers degrees of separation. It differed from the poor immigrant children illegally crossing the border from Mexico into the United States, promising a better life. Those children hardly stood a chance; regardless, their families had to pay a hefty price. Many were raped and sometimes killed by the people leading them across the border, and the U.S. did nothing to stop it—thoughts for another day.

What would the USMC think of the Commander's affiliation with the cartels and the money he made for looking the other way? He needed assurance, and the only way to achieve his purpose was to exterminate Vicarelli by any means, and the best way to flush him out was through Trinity.

Since Babe and the boys didn't have high-tech communication like the intruders most likely had, they devised an alternate method. Each boy had a pen light and would flash it once to say mission accomplished or twice if they missed their target. Whatever the case, they were to advance. Babe speculated fireflies would camouflage a quick flash of a pen light.

The plan was Judd would take out the first driver and perhaps the passenger as well, definitely disabling the vehicle. The second SUV would likely pick up speed and go around the incapacitated first vehicle. The boys would lay roofing tacks along the road, hoping to compromise the tires of the second vehicle, and if not, they'd shoot them out. Babe advised that the intruders would likely evacuate the vehicle and proceed on foot. The last car, he speculated, would remain at the edge of the property and be used as transport back to the city since the other two were rendered useless. If there were more than three vehicles, Babe told them to back off and skirt the outside of the property through the pastures, then cover the mud room door outside if necessary. Babe would be on the roof and knew he could pick most of them off. The ones who escaped, he would deal with in a hand-to-hand confrontation.

Armed with a shotgun and a couple of holstered pistols, Paul would stay in the hallway in front of the hidden safe room occupied by Inez and Trinity. He anchored a rope to the bed for the two women to climb down if they set the house ablaze. He wondered if Deary would send more people than the five from earlier.

PICKED THE WRONG FIGHT

*W*aiting for hell to let loose, Inez fixed sandwiches. The men were gathered in the living room going over the plans, each understanding their role and the danger involved. They heard crackles from tires on the gravel, although it was still daylight. Inez peered out the window. It was an unmarked police unit with two officers; the boys identified them as Darren and Beau. Judd hailed them and pointed to the barn.

What would the logical placement be for the officers? Babe would decide when he came from upstairs. Big Paul called him down, Trinity trotting behind him. The deputies candidly said they were off-duty, and it was their choice to join in the movie-like gunfight. While said in a joking manner, both understood the severity of the situation. The confrontation was no picnic in the park, and in all likelihood, they would lose one or two from either side.

After everything was said and done, Babe would be on the Commander like stink on shit. All the drama had gone too far, involving way too many lives. Why couldn't he have just called Babe and talked it through? If Deary wasn't profiting from his relationship with the cartel at the risk of others, Babe had no qualms with the interaction; hell, his girlfriend's dad was a mobster of sorts, and one day, he might be married to the Mob. It didn't mean he would play their games or have any involvement. Babe figured he had a mission of his own to follow.

The sun started to set; Trinity hugged tightly to her Marine. "Don't you go trying to be a hero and get yourself hurt. You already have a hole in your hip; let it heal, and for Heaven's sake, you don't need any more. No more, my man." She poked her finger into his chest, emphasizing her point.

Babe scaled the house and positioned himself on the roof. He had a good view of the entrance, the gravel drive, the surrounding trees, and the dense foliage skirting the property. He spotted one deputy camouflaged in the brush. They had no intention of trying to solve the issue without violence. They had come to fight. He wondered if the Sheriff was privy to their preferences or had it been another impossible lie. In the conversation leading up to getting in position, he learned both deputies had been Army. When they heard the perpetrators were rogue military, their feathers became more than ruffled. It was a blemish on the fighting men and women of the U.S. Armed Forces. It had become personal, and Babe understood the sentiment.

One car pulled onto the gravel road with the headlights off. *Boom-Boom.* Two quick and thunderous shots from Judd eliminated the first threat. He flashed his penlight once—targets taken down. As Babe figured, the second car flew past the oaks with headlights on high beam. He saw the flash burst from inside the SUV. Two people rolled out of the back of the vehicle and traveled on foot, forking off from each other. *Pop.* A smaller gun downed one of the men, but the SUV kept going with determination. A third car moved with speed, followed by a fourth. Someone shot the tires out of the fourth car. Then, a series of rapid-fire commenced, and the gunfight was officially in action. Flashes of light from gun muzzles lit the night. He saw two pen lights quickly flash with a singular pulse.

One of the intruders made it to within three hundred yards. Babe took the shot, and the person went down permanently. The bodies running crouched low and seemed like ants coming from a mound. They had automatic weapons and were skilled, but the young boys stayed hidden, only stepping out to take one down. They knew how to cover each other. Three people ran toward the house. Darren and Beau tackled two while Babe took out the other. He quickly jumped to the ground from the porch roof, knowing the deputies would probably be unprepared for the two they wrestled. Babe entered the fight, crushing the windpipe of one and slicing the other's throat, but a few more were approaching and opened up on them. They dove into the ditch, crawling on their stomachs, staying low but closing in on their targets undetected. One person stopped short. Judd had climbed from the tree, carefully approached, and took the shot. The front of the person blew out as the shotgun blast ripped through them. Babe had no idea how many were left.

A shot came from the backyard. Minutes later, there were flashes from the upstairs window, one after the other. Big Paul was the only one upstairs with a gun. One of the boys was close to the house, but Babe took off at top speed, entered the house with stealth, and saw a person slowly and silently climbing the stairs. Just as quietly, he slipped behind him and torqued his neck, quietly lowering him to the floor. Babe continued up. The sounds of hand-to-hand combat echoed down the hall. The man got a chokehold on Paul. Occupied with trying to take Big Paul down, Babe fired one well-placed shot, hitting the man in the eye, which lessened the hold as he fell backward. Paul took one of his holstered revolvers and shot the man square in the face and neck. Babe motioned to him to stay upstairs with Inez and Trinity.

Slowly, Babe crept down the stairs when a woman he recognized came through the door blazing. For a brief moment, she paused; seeing him, he took advantage and pumped two shots into her. Blood drooled from the corner of her mouth. He stood over her. The words rang through his mind: *live or die.* She gurgled out in a low, strained whisper, "Vic?"

"Nothing personal, Ingram," he popped another round into her with a fatal shot. He exited through the mudroom.

"I think we got them all 'cept one Judd hogtied him. We figured you'd want to talk to him—all total dead: six men and a couple of females. Babe thought, *not counting Ingram or the hogtied assailant.* Oh yeah, he wanted to talk to him. "Judd's dragging him to the house."

"Make it the barn, son." Babe headed out the door toward the barn. He didn't want a chance of Trinity seeing the carnage. "Y'all need to dig a deep hole. Lay the bodies out; I want to look at them and maybe take a picture or two for their boss." Thoughts chased in his mind. He wondered how many of the dead did he serve with or know. Darren and Beau approached, sweat running down the sides of their faces.

"Holy shit," Darren exclaimed with animation, "You musta pissed somebody off bad. They sent ten killers, wow—you some kinda mean motherfucker—'portant to someone, dude. I'll remember tonight and stay well out your way." Babe nodded but wanted to say it wasn't his choice. They picked a fight with him. The young country boys were more than up to the task and took care of business like they'd been in combat for years.

After dragging the one left alive and lining up the dead, Babe shot pictures of them all and threw them into the gaping hole. "One of you mind jumping in the tractor and shoveling the dirt over the hole? Y'all dug a fuckin' canyon. Anyone got jumper cables? The older boy shrugged and said he'd get it for him; he fetched it and brought it to Babe, who headed to the barn.

By this time, the police were long gone, and a man, tied in knotted rope, lay huddled on his side in the middle of the barn. Babe kicked him over. "Well, fuck me. Stu Pepper, what the hell you doing in this mess?" The man's one good eye bulged out as he strained to see in the dark; the other was swollen shut and unable to see anything. "I thought you were out on a medical discharge, and now you're PMC? Somebody fucked you hard, getting you to go into the private sector. Sgt. Pepper a Personal Military Contractor. What the fuck?"

Stu Pepper kept silent for a few minutes.

"You got nothin' to say?" Babe sarcastically asked. "What was your assignment? What you say determines the next course of action, so pick your words wisely." He towered over the man, intensifying the level of insecurity and fear.

Blood dripped from the corner of Stu's mouth; he had scrapes and was worn pitiful from an intense beating. "Our assignment was to extract a hostage at this location."

"Bullshit. The assignment was more like y'all taking a hostage." Babe countered.

"Believe what you want; you're going to anyway, but I swear." He hesitated, then asked. "What the hell are you doing here, anyway?"

"Protecting my woman."

Silence.

"If you're gonna kill me, fuckin' do it. I was doing this as a favor to the Commander. Yeah, we were getting paid, but not what we usually get paid by oil companies or private firms." Babe could usually tell when someone was lying, and his bullshit-o-meter hadn't sounded. His gut said the guy was telling the truth. He had gotten maneuvered like a pawn on a chessboard; Babe was familiar with Deary's M.O. *That's what trust gets you,* he thought.

"Your team's dead, Pep. You're the only one left." His statement was blunt, to the point, with no inflection of emotion.

Babe cut the rope holding him. In the man's condition, one sharp blow would have taken him out; besides, there was far more to gain with him being kept alive. Babe asked him to explain in detail what the Commander had said. He then devised a plan. He'd get Stu to call the Commander arrange a meet, and instead of delivering Trinity, he'd get a bigger surprise. "Man, I don't know if I can do it without him figuring it out—you're asking me for the impossible, Vic. Lie to the Commander; he'll know. He's crafty, the old bird."

Babe pulled up two rusty metal folding chairs. "Picture this. Chop, you remember him," the guy nodded, "comes home and starts running drugs and trafficking kids for the cartel." Stu's mouth dropped. "Oh, no, there's more. He comes to where my lady works, pretending he's looking for me because his old lady ran off or whatever. Can I help him? Some explanation, right? No, motherfucker, what he came to Louie's for was to scope out Trinity, my girl, who he'd planned to traffick earlier and was chasing it up. He probably shit his pants when he saw me and made up some bullshit story, which didn't seem right at the time, but the asshole saved my ass too many times to refuse. Bottom line, after I think it's all over and the cops have him, it wasn't. Weeks later, I'm going to my place with Trinity; he and some other piece of shit jump me with a stun gun, drug me, and take me to his boss, a cartel guy. This dude says, 'Your loyalty or your life.' Fuck, Trinity's the only one that gives a hearty shit about me, so I tell him I don't know him to pledge my loyalty. Who shows themselves but the Commander and gives me the nod, you know, the nod, to work with the guy. The story continues, but to wind it up, after a few months living with the cartel, the guy tells me that the Commander wants me dead and I can't return to New Orleans. I say, fuck that, fuck the Commander and the horse he rode in on. Pep, Deary knows he can't find me and decides to kidnap my girl to flush me out. To me, he signed a death warrant. It's either him or me; frankly, I'm not ready to depart, especially to a treasonous bastard like him. I'm gonna kill the motherfucker. Now you can help me, or a man's gotta do what a man's gotta do, nothing personal."

Pep hadn't blinked and sat with a look of disbelief and shock hearing Babe's story. "I'm in with you, Vic. What bullshit. Yeah, I can lie; that's fucked up. I'll tell him I have the girl and tell him whatever you want." He looked as sincere as he could for someone with a blown-up lip and only one functional eye. Judd had kicked the crap out of him, and the eye was black and swollen closed, possibly damaged for life. "The man's gone sideways. Power has gotten to his head; it happens, I suppose."

They walked to the house. By this time, Trinity was in the living room, Inez was in the kitchen bandaging Paul, and the boys were hanging on the front porch trash-talking each other about the shoot-out. According to each, they saved the day with their intense skills.

Babe explained to the rogue Marine he needed to meet the Commander somewhere in Gretna. Pep could walk away none the wiser with a pocket full of cash.

He quieted the room while Stu called. "Deal is done." Babe clearly noted the lack of a 'sir' from Stu to Deary. In itself, it spoke volumes. No matter how angry one might be with a superior officer, one would always acknowledge the rank with a 'sir.' "We'll be at the Off-Track Betting place by the Casino after you cross the bridge into Gretna. We'll get there by zero-three-hundred."

Babe texted Antoine Sr.: Sorry for the time. I got her, and all is well. Paul bringing her home soon.

Antoine texted back a thumb-up.

Trinity moved like a cat, sleek and silent with a sultriness that sent waves of heat through his body. "Boy, lemme take a look. You ruined your shirt, and it's my favorite denim shirt on you. We'll get you another one, or I'll try my Mama's stain-removing solution. She concocts a little of this and a little of that, then tops it with a crust of salt." Trinity shrugged her shoulders. "Maybe I'll get her to do it," and laughed. "Now, Babe, Paul is in no condition to drive, so I'm gonna be his driver tonight or this morning. It's one-ten." She looked under his shirt, went into the kitchen, grabbed some gauze, and cleaned his oozing wound. "Babe Vicarelli, I hope you can take a quick minute and stay out of trouble."

He said he'd see her at her place before sunrise and would she take Gunner.

"You mean hero extraordinaire," she smiled.

Babe cocked his head to the side, similar to Gunner. "What?" Trinity told him the dog flattened and held the throat of the first person who tried to come into the house—the man who shot Li'l Hank, the redhead. He hadn't realized any of their people had injuries. Trinity let him know Judd sustained a ricochet in his thigh from a chunk of wood, but Inez had already seen to it, and only one other hand got hit, Li'l Hank.

All in all, it was a miracle. At least ten combat-trained people were on the attacking team, and the home team had farm hands, two local cops, a bodyguard, Inez, Trinity, and himself, not forgetting Gunner. They came through victorious with the odds stacked against them, thankfully no mortalities on their side.

Inez was still busy patching up Paul in the kitchen. "You okay?" Babe asked.

"I will be. Things could have been a lot worse. Your timing was perfect." He explained the plan to Paul, said he'd be leaving shortly, and Paul should return Trinity to the city. "Hey, give your girl a little attention. She is freaked." The puncture from the bullet in his hip was far from healed, and the excitement of the night's drama jarred whatever plug had started forming. Once Trinity dressed his wound, Babe held her, kissing the top of her head.

"Life will get back to our normal; you'll see." She nodded but had a curious look of doubt in her eyes. "It will. Maybe not everyone else's normal, but ours."

Babe questioned if Pep was ready to go. "Yep, you know what they say about payback. The Commander won't be able to squeak through this one." If anything, he seemed to perk up, like he was looking forward to the encounter.

Trinity drove them from the house to the only functioning vehicle from their parade of SUVs. It sat parked at the end of the gravel road. As they approached, their headlights lit up the car. "There's somebody in the car. How many people did y'all bring," he asked Pep.

"Twelve. Why?"

"We only got ten, which means we have two more roaming the property, or they're in there." He pointed straight ahead. "At least one of them is." He told Trinity to stop, let them out, and make tracks to the house. "This feels like a never-ending nightmare." They approached the vehicle as though they were two of the unit from the assignment. The closer they got, it became apparent both were inside the car."

Stu led. "What are y'all doing here? What's up with Rusty?"

Babe heard one voice, "There's no y'all. Rusty is dead, and they shot me to shit. The country police ambushed us on their way out. Y'all find the girl, Stu?"

A low rumble started in Babe's innermost being erupting like a volcano, "No, you stupid motherfucker." He picked up speed, yanked open the door, and grabbed the injured man by the scruff of his neck. The guy yelled out to Babe. "Captain, it's me, Texas." Babe already had his fist drawn, ready to cold-cock the man, but stopped. He could feel the quiver in Texas' body. "What the hell are you doing here? If I woulda known you had anything to do with this, I would never have agreed—" No doubt the Commander had fed some bullshit story about a girl they needed to save.

Stu explained to Texas, telling him the story Deary had fed them was horseshit, and the actual situation was FUBAR. They checked the man's injuries, and he would hold until Stu could get him treated after collecting the money and dropping Babe off. The conclusion was the Commander had gone off the tracks, way off, like he had lost his mind. The entire exercise was a scheme to flush out the Captain; the girl was collateral damage. Hearing Trinity referred to as collateral damage fueled explosions in his gut. The sooner they got on the road, the better. Babe called Trinity. "Let the boys know we have another body. It'll be in the ditch at the end of the road. There were twelve, and now all are accounted for. We are heading to the city, and I'll see you at your place. This whole fucking mess will be behind us. I love you, girl."

The entire ride to the city, Babe planned how the meet with Deary would go. There were so many things he wanted to say to him, but the thoughts all sounded like a whiny bitch, and that was not how he viewed himself. The soundtrack he ran in his head was people do what they feel they have to in order to survive; after all, that was what life was about, right? Survival. Sometimes, what they perceived was far from accurate; for example, he had no interest in what the Commander was up to as long as no one was getting hurt. It was their duty to fight for those too weak to fight, punish those needing punishment, and eliminate threats—actual threats, the kind that hurt the innocent. The Marines had ingrained it in them, and Deary held that high standard, even higher than his Staff Sargeant, which was almost unattainable.

Given the hour, the Causeway, I-10, and the Expressway were easy to maneuver with light traffic. Texas was in no condition to get out of the vehicle when they met Deary. Tremors began in Babe's belly as they crossed the Crescent City Connection over the Mississippi River. Looking out, it was a peaceful view with the lights glimmering from the city and ships navigating through the water at a snail's pace.

As soon as he ended Deary's crazy delusions, the better off everyone would be. He knew finding Deary's body would be plastered all over the news, and knowing his status as a Marine kind of guy, he'd bet the farm Trey and Max would bend his ear about the Commander. It was bound to happen. Once again, he flirted with the idea that he could pull off what was needed to stay clear of the commotion. The thing was, both Stu and Texas would know, and it could bite him in the ass one day. He stopped the vehicle before getting to the Off Track Betting and Casino.

"Pep, how cool are you with this?" He watched every minute movement, shift of the eyes, and flex of the body. From all accounts, Babe did not perceive any threat. Texas, if he lived, might be a different story.

He thumbed to the rear seat. "And?" Pep shrugged, tilting his head to the side.

"Your guess is as good as mine. Captain, do what you gotta do. I understand the loose-end theory, but I give you my word; I'll help in the deed, making me equal in responsibility as you." Babe started with probing questions like what was the worst assignment he ever had and what kept him up at night or etched into his nightmares. Those essential ticket items sketched the picture of the man. The question was, did Babe risk all in trusting him? Trust so far in life had given him nothing but a sour, very sour taste. They pulled out and went to the OTB, backing into a deserted parking lot area hidden in the darkness and shadowed corner. He disabled the interior light, stepped out of the car, and opened the rear door. He leaned in and told Texas it wasn't personal and broke the man's neck with a tight twist. It wasn't exhilarating; if anything, it was depressing. It was all for self-preservation and the promise, albeit maybe an empty promise, of a chance at an uncomplicated life. The deed was self-serving, against his philosophy.

Deary pulled next to the SUV. Stu walked to the driver's side. "Money first, then the girl. We lost everyone but me."

"You look like hell. Your money is in the trunk." How perfect was that going to be with the trunk opened? Something smelled rotten, and if he were to guess, he bet Deary was going to eliminate Pep. *Not on my watch*, he smirked. Deary was first to the popped-open trunk, reached in on the pretense of grabbing the money, but came up with a pistol. "Sorry, son, no loose ends. Nothing personal." Babe came from behind and, with all his might, slammed Deary's shoulder with his fist, making him lose the weapon.

"You piece of shit," Babe growled.

"Wait, Vicarelli, what are you doing?" The Commander's eyes bugged out, and he tried to say he was the good guy.

"I can't say it's not personal because motherfucker it doesn't get any closer than this. See you in Hell, Commander." He used the pistol he'd picked up from the ground and shot directly into the deceiver's heart, pushing his body into the trunk. "Pep, follow me. We're gonna make this look like another one of the Westbank murders. Then drop me on Rampart and Iberville." He took the duffel bag of money. "It's yours when you drop me on Rampart. Dump Texas in the East and torch him."

Stu walked to the vehicle and followed Babe in the Commander's car under the bridge a few streets from the levee close to the old Fischer project, which the city tore down and reconstructed. The police had found the other three murder victims close by. *Done.* Babe had used his shirt sleeves as gloves on the steering wheel to avoid fingerprints. There wasn't any evidence implicating him. The ride to Rampart was quiet until Pep spoke. "You knew he was going to kill me, didn't you? I guess it makes sense there was no one else left alive to point the finger at him. I guess I shouldn't have told him everyone was dead."

With a half-sided smile, Babe chuffed an amused breath. "After seeing what I had and hearing what he'd said, I knew the old bastard wouldn't leave any loose ends. He would have figured out a way to eliminate all of you or compromise you so much you would be indebted to him forever. I'll be interested to hear what the news has to say about the discovery. I don't usually watch it; it pisses me off."

"Me neither. The fucking way things are handled now with the military, at least to the public, is sickening. You know, over half of what they say is bullshit. The Marine Corps is strong as ever, maybe underfunded, and like always, they weed out the ones who aren't Corps material. You were right. I had a medical discharge, but it was more psych than anything, and I think it's something only time might lessen; it'll never go away completely. Thanks, Captain, you saved my ass one more time." He pulled up to the corner of Iberville and Rampart.

"Hey, Marine, it was mine to do." There was a slight satisfaction in completing the Deary mission, but it also wrenched him a bit. He remembered Javier's question. *Could he kill Deary? Answer: Yes, but it stung.*

CAN WE BREATHE NOW?

*T*he whole way walking to Trinity's, he thought about the future and what it might look like. Was he prepared to be that guy who went to church with her family every Sunday, supposedly praying to a God he wasn't sure existed? He knew he'd had strong feelings for her from the moment he saw her, and it wasn't just the heat below his belt. She awakened something in him that had never been alive. The question remained: Was he a good enough human being to be the man she needed? It was more about what was good for her. He'd gotten by for a long time without someone in his life. Being on his own was natural; it was a steady relationship he found strange. He figured they had been an item for over seven months, closer to nine, and during their time together, it had been one drama after another—some his and some hers. Was life always going to be a page out of the movies? *Is that how ordinary people live—from one drama to another?* Neither of them was basic Jane or Joe.

Babe thought about his ball of beautiful, sexy energy. She, in herself, was a contradiction, creating uneasy feelings within her family. The Noelles were a prominent family, the upper crust, yet their baby girl loved tending bar and entertaining the late-night crowd. It certainly wasn't par for the course. And what about him? Maybe he should have stayed in the Marine Corps; he didn't do well without a purpose, structure, or rules of engagement; he made his own standards while ambling through civilian life. People who took advantage of others because of weakness, inept intelligence, or gullibility deserved what they had coming. As he saw it, it was his primary purpose; construction was his pay-the-bills job, but above and beyond everything was Trinity.

The French Quarter, despite some of the ne'er-do-wells, was enchanting and lured people of every age, culture, and demographic. Calling it home hadn't been part of his plan, but since the shrinks told him repeatedly to be active and engage in social interaction, he thought it was the place to immerse into civilian life. There were plenty of people; there was always something to do and a palette of outlandishness to keep his mind occupied, which for him was as essential as breathing. The quiet brought out his demons.

Babe never intended to fall in love, get married, or have a family—with his dysfunctional upbringing, it was no surprise. Having female company and meeting particular needs hadn't been an issue. Walking into Louie's that evening changed everything when he spied the exotically gorgeous Creole bartender. Her affability took him by surprise and created a magnetic pull, keeping her ever-present in his mind. He didn't anticipate the possibility of awakening what he thought were non-existent emotions; nevertheless, the Marine was drowning in a sea of feelings he wasn't equipped to handle. He stalled any engagement in conversation merely observing her, not that he was ever one for much socializing, anyway. Giving commands or communicating orders was hardly socializing. But, after it was said and done, he was most definitely in love with Miss Trinity Noelle.

Walking into the lobby of Hotel Noelle had started to feel comfortable, but it seemed like a lifetime ago. "Good morning, Mr. Vicarelli; long time no see." *Mr. Vicarelli?* He had gotten to know Lex, the night manager, well. So much had happened in the time he and Trinity had been together. *Mr. Vicarelli, indeed.* What was wrong with the picture? Did he think Babe had skipped out on the girl and left her heartbroken? If that were the case, he'd get to the bottom of it and sort it all out. He didn't choose to be away from her, at least for the most part.

To be an ass and display the absurdity of the interaction, Babe said, "Yes, good morning, Lexington," with an exaggerated English lilt. The man behind the counter looked at him, startled by the exchange. Babe went to the counter. "I've been gone too long; it's good to be home, and please, I know you haven't forgotten, use my name. Has my lady gotten back yet?" Lex nodded exuberantly, making up for the stodgy welcome. Babe smiled and headed toward her apartment. He could hear Gunner howling when he turned toward the door. "Okay, Gunn, settle down. Shh," he called from the hallway.

Trinity flung the door open, letting Gunner race out to him. He grabbed her around the waist, hugged her, and then gave Gunner much-desired attention. She pulled Babe along by the hand. Once inside the apartment, she bathed him in kisses. "The nightmare is over, amen. You've got to be beat; get your ass in bed. You need sleep, my man." She stopped him, checked his puncture, washed some of the ooze off, and lay beside him in the bed. "I'm not gonna ask because I don't want to know, but things are gonna be normal like you said?" He nodded, pulling her close and cradling her body like spoons in a drawer.

A few hours passed, and he was sleeping so soundly that his breaths were long and deep, like he had passed out. In the distance, almost like part of a dream, he could hear Trinity on the phone. "Yes, Finn, we'll be back into the routine tonight. No more disappearing acts, I promise. The Hulk is fine. See you at work tonight. He's gonna totally be awed by our performance; I can't wait." She hung up with him and started talking to herself as she busied in the kitchen and turned the TV on low. "Oh, yeah, my man's gonna want a piece of this when he sees the show. She started practicing with the bottles and then moved on to dancing in the living room as though she were on the bartop. Her movements were naturally sultry, but with an exaggerated panache, they were downright steamy and erotic. Babe quietly stood in her doorway and watched as her body writhed to the music playing in her head. At one point, she pivoted and saw him standing, watching her with a smile. "How long you been there?" She put her hand on her hip and giggled, falling onto the sofa. Although silent, the Commander's picture flashed on the television. She turned it up.

The newscaster spoke in the same monotone voice as though announcing the winner of the Girl Scout cookie sale. "Another strike by the serial killer. The latest victim, Commander G.R.Deary, a Marine officer of distinction, serving our country during his illustrious career for many years, was found shot to death blocks away from the last victim. His murder makes four strikes in three weeks. Anyone with any information, please call the hotline at the bottom of your screen." He went on to give a complete description of Commander Deary's service.

"Turn it off," Babe asked. He knew it wouldn't be long before he'd get calls or some contact from Trey or Max out of curiosity. "So," he pulled her up from the sofa, holding her close, their bodies touching, "What you got going on at Louie's tonight? Am I going to like this? I don't want to have to play bouncer keeping roving hands off you."

Trinity pulled away and looked into his eyes, "Big man, have I ever needed you to protect me at Louie's? Boy, I got this under control. I want you to sit back, enjoy, and know most of my moves are for you." She touched her tongue to the tip of her finger and put it on her expressive hip movement while making a sizzling sound. "You'll feel my heat, big man."

He raised an eyebrow. "And I won't want to knock anyone's block off?"

She laughed, "Nah, it's all in good fun."

"Yeah, all fun and games until—"

She put her hand up. "Well, brother, if you can't deal with it, then don't come, but I think you'll be just fine."

It had been months since Babe had been on the job site. He brought Trinity and Gunner as well. Babe didn't want to be away from her or his dog for a second. From what he could tell, the project was near completion as they pulled up on site. "Well, I'll be damned; you do have a vehicle." Glenn laughed as he put his hand out to shake Babes. "From what I hear, you've been through hell and back. Thanks for bringing my stepson," he reached, fluffing Gunner's fur. "Start anytime you like; it'll be good to have you on the job. We have another project on Conti. I got the plans in the office. We should finish here within the next two to three weeks, but if you could get the Conti one started, that would be great, if you want. You can finish here if it's what you prefer or whatever works with your availability."

Babe could see some of the guys on the site eyeing Trinity. He couldn't blame them; she was beautiful. They all seemed to have the good sense not to wolf whistle, cat call, or 'hey baby' her.

"I'll be here bright and early tomorrow, and we can review what you want. I'm hoping nothing takes me away from work again for a long time." He gave a half-smile. "You were our first stop; I wanted to make sure I still had a job. We are going to her mom's, and she's going to work, so on a tight schedule. Glad to know I still work here." Glenn patted him on the back, commenting again he'd always have a job with him. Babe couldn't help but think he'd have never put up with someone so unreliable. Even knowing all the facts, Babe was pretty sure Glenn didn't and was stretching out on a limb. He hoped the message hadn't come from her dad.

Trinity climbed up in the truck, and Gunner jumped into the back seat. The next stop would be her parent's home. Babe called her dad. "Hello, sir. All is well, and we're heading to see your wife. I appreciate your help, sir." Getting assistance from anyone was a difficult thing for him, but especially help from Trinity's dad. Had the gesture come with a price? Was it a price he was willing to pay? Babe hoped no strings were attached because it would become a big problem and an impossible lie for him.

Trinity's mom clutched him in a death grip like he was her long lost son. "I have been praying the Rosary for you, honey." She said to him. *What am I supposed to say?* "Our girl was torn up. She prayed the Rosary and went to St. Dominic's almost every day. Nothing can beat the power of prayer and the merciful love of God." She smiled and squeezed his hand.

All he could do was say 'yes, ma'am' and nod. The woman was as lovely as could be and most caring, but he wanted to get out as fast as possible. The whole huggy kissy thing made him uncomfortable, more than uneasy. *Would you say you have intimacy issues?* He recalled one doctor asking him; he chuckled inside because the answer set ol' doc back when he responded. *Hell no, I can fuck just about any hot woman, and sometimes they don't even have to be that hot. He winked at the doctor, who sat with his mouth agape.*

"Mama, Babe wanted to say hi, and I needed a hug, but I have work tonight, so we gotta skate. I need a few things I left here." She went into her bedroom, and Babe followed. As she rummaged through drawers and the closet, he looked around the room with an amused half-smile.

"So this is where Trinity grew up? Somehow, it looks like you, and I can imagine you as a little girl throwing temper tantrums, humming your dolls, and screaming at your parents." He laughed.

"Who told you that?" She defensively prodded.

"No one; I know you and your spicy hot temper. I bet you were a mouthy thing, am I right? I bet Bethany was sweet and quiet, obeyed the rules, and didn't sass. Am I close?" She threw one of her headscarves at him.

Standing with hands on her hips and a scowl on her face, Trinity responded. "You got a lot of nerve, coming in my bedroom, judging me, and then," and she changed her voice to a higher pitch, "Poor Bethany, the good girl, who never did anything wrong. I see how it is." He scooped her up like a toy doll.

"My girl, I wouldn't want you any other way. I'm dickin' with you. I love my feisty girl." He swatted her on the butt. "Now let's move; you have to get to work, and I have to go to Chestnut to check on the boys."

Babe dropped her at the hotel and headed toward St. Charles Avenue with Gunner. He wondered how things were going with the addition of Jacob. He hoped the other boys wouldn't gang up on him but imagined Ruthie would have them by the balls if they did; she didn't put up with much nonsense. It was good for them. She was fair and kind but ruled no question about it.

As the truck came to a halt, Gunner sprinted into the backyard. Jacob was outside, picked up one of the squeaky toys, and tossed it for the dog. It was a great game, and Gunner seemed to bask in the attention. There was nothing quite like a young boy with a dog. They were both filled with a roughhouse spirit. "Things okay for you here, kid?" The boy grinned and nodded. "Where's everybody else?"

Jacob squeezed the toy and held it up so Gunner had to jump. "Reg is in time-out, and Chris," the boy rolled his eyes, "Is on the phone with his girlfriend, Brooke." Babe nodded. Chris, a teenager, was already into relationships, even if they were fleeting and superficial. *Good for him*, he thought; *he might have a chance at a normal life.*

Ruthie called Babe. "Glad you're here. I need you to talk to trouble with a capital T." Babe skipped a step and responded to her beckon.

"What's up?"

"That boy of yours, Reg, has a mouth like a sailor. Now, I know boys will be boys, but I don't expect them to use foul kind of language in front of me. No sir." She shook her head with vehemence, wagging her finger.

"Yes, ma'am. On it." Babe took the stairs two at a time, then heard a distinct clearing of Ruthie's throat. He stopped running but had to chuckle inside. He walked into the bedroom. "Reg, what's up? Have you been sassing Ruthie?"

Reg popped up off the bed. "No. She's mad at me—here's the story. Her son Clive gave me a bike. Some stupid motherfucker jumped our fence and took the bike. I saw him out the window and ran after him, but he was too fast. I yelled at him. I told him he was a cocksucking motherfucker, then the next thing I know, Ruthie grabs my ear and drags me up the stairs saying those kinds of words were the words of the devil." Babe couldn't help but think he'd probably have said the same thing but understood Ruthie was trying to rear them properly.

"You know where the kid lives that stole the bike?"

"Kinda. The boy's name is Lamar, and he rides the same school bus, so maybe not exact, but close enough." Babe held his chuckle inside so as not to thwart Ruthie's discipline.

"Let's go get your bike." Reg slipped into his Nikes and pulled his jeans lower on his hips. Babe shook his head. "You lookin' to get fucked in the ass?" The boy's eyes popped out like they were on springs.

"Uh, no."

"Well, wearing your pants like that is telling the world you want it up the ass." The boy quickly pulled his pants up a few inches. Babe nodded. The two went down the stairs; the big guy told Ruthie Reg had something to say, and then they would get the bike."

"I'm sorry, Miss Ruthie. I shouldn't have said those words in front of you." Reg batted his eyes like an innocent doe—*bullshit artist*. Ruthie accepted the apology and hugged the boy, telling him it was good to apologize.

The big man and small boy left the yard, Reg giving Babe directions. Three blocks over, a few kids were playing ball in the front yard with said bike thrown to the side. Reg went to get the bike, but Babe stopped him, and they went to the door. After a few knocks, an attractive woman, maybe early forties, answered the door. "Can I help you?"

"Perhaps, ma'am." Babe tried his best at cordial friendly, but it was not his best suit. "I think one of these boys borrowed Reg's bike, and he needs to get it back. I told him not to take it but to ask your permission." She glared at one of the boys.

"Who took this boy's bike?" She demanded.

Babe put his hand up to stop her, knowing it would make matters worse. Reg jumped in, "No one took it, ma'am. They wanted to borrow it, that's all." It was apparent to Babe who the bully was, and he could see a sigh of relief on the boy's face.

"If you say so, son." Reg had not convinced the mom, but he played the role perfectly. "By all means, please take your bike. Lamar had his stolen last week, and we haven't had a chance to get him a new one yet. How nice of you." She turned to Babe, "I'm Janie Miller, and you are?"

"Sorry, ma'am, I'm Babe Vicarelli. I have a house a few blocks away. We have three boys as well." She smiled with a flirt on her face. She glanced at his left hand, taking note of no ring. *I will rectify this.* They said farewell; Reg got the bike, straddling it as they walked the rest of the way to the house. As soon as they got to the house, Babe ran upstairs and grabbed one of the diamond rings from the brown leather case. He knew it would swallow Trinity, but he'd have it sized the best he could and get one of the rubber rings for his hand—*no more unsolicited gestures.*

Ruthie was preparing dinner and asked if Babe would be joining them. He did. Chat at the dinner table commenced after Ruthie made the boys say grace. They fought for words with him, each vying for the big guy's attention. After an hour of shooting the breeze with the boys, he called them outside on the porch. "No more cursing in front of Ruthie. If I can refrain, then you little motherfuckers should be able to." The boys belly laughed. "Got it?" They all agreed. "What you say to each other quietly is your business. I don't want to hear about it at school, in front of Ruthie, or on the bus. Y'all feeling what I'm sayin?" They nodded. "Oh, and keep the bike in the garage, but don't scratch the car."

It felt good to spend time with the boys. At some point, he wanted to talk to Jacob about his experience in Cartagena. He watched Reg put the bike in the garage and then reversed out of the driveway.

He was two minutes into the ride to the Quarter when his phone rang. "Vicarelli."

"Vic, hey man, it's Hurley. How's it hangin'? You home from all your camping? Blew my mind when your girl told me. I figured you'd had enough sleeping under the stars." He chuckled. "I know I have." Of all the people he served with, Hurley was the one who had been through the most dangerous missions with him. It's not like they were friends, but closer than he was to most people.

"Things are good. What's up? I know this isn't a social call."

"You're right, sir. I'm working with a Marine named Pierce Kelly. He served for one, maybe two tours. He's with the feds now and has been for some time. It's a good gig, and I know he's looking for more men. Your name came to my mind first."

"Is it for strong arm stuff, bodyguard, or lengthy missions?"

"No strong arm or missions. It's bodyguard duty for celebrities and politicians at prime events inside the U.S. The job is for one or two-nighters, all expenses paid, and the pay is like a five hundred dollar per diem. Such low pay tells you it's not edgy; it's a walk in the park, Cap. If the exposure and challenge were more significant, the money would be a shit-ton, like in the thousands a day. Before you say no, talk to the guy. You'd be great at it." Was it worth looking into? The only bodyguard thing he'd ever done turned out to be a fucking fiasco and not the easy no-action detail described. It's not like anyone promised it would be a slam dunk, but it kept him away from Trinity and took much longer than expected. Besides, he got shot, and the damn thing hadn't healed yet. Maybe if he sat his ass out of some of the chaos, he could have a subdued life, and the fucking thing would have a chance to mend.

"I just got in town, as you know, but sure, we can meet, and I'll hear your guy out but gotta go. Later." Babe fiddled with the ring in his pocket. Could he say, 'Here, wear this, but it doesn't mean anything yet?' No. He needed to be clever about it. A light bulb switched on over his head. Maybe slip it on her finger while sleeping; *nah, chicken shit.*

Out of the blue, he flashed back to a memory he'd created. There were hoards of children who had been abducted and packed like sardines in a hot, dirty warehouse. He hadn't seen it for himself, but it was the image he conjured. He needed to free them, not only one or two. How many? It was a thirty-plus billion-dollar industry, according to Javier. Rather than babysit the spoiled rich and famous, he'd prefer to follow a cause, but how?

Before anything, he'd talk it over with Trinity; she had a right to weigh in as the owner of his heart.

Babe could hear the hoopla from Louie's blocks away. He rounded the corner in time to see Finn lift Trinity onto the bar. Her dancing was fun, and if someone's dick was getting hard, it wasn't because of her moves; it was maybe not family-friendly, but not like riding a pole. She was right; it was fun, and everyone was having a good time. There wasn't anyone he wanted to knock out. Finn held her hand when she came off the bar like a princess, and the two worked the bar like nothing he'd seen before. They were having fun along with the throngs of people lined up at the bar. For grins, he glanced to his usual seat, and sure enough, she had a reserved sign holding his place.

Babe moved his way through the crowd to his bar stool. Finn raised his chin to Trinity, who looked over and winked at him. It didn't take but a few minutes before he had his two-finger pour of Glenlivet. She quickly ran over to him. "Food?"

"Already eaten with Ruthie and the boys." She nodded. He sat watching the mayhem, knowing her performance was for him. Those were her words, right? He couldn't help but chuckle, watching the duo behind the bar. It wasn't like a band with breaks between sets. It was nonstop for hours on end. As the night progressed and the clock ticked to midnight, he knew he needed to tuck in for the night. Babe winked at her and left a ten on the bar top. She blew him a kiss. There was too much commotion for her to stop and run around the bar like before to kiss him goodnight.

Walking to the hotel, he felt the presence of someone approaching. He quickly turned and shouted, "Not tonight!" To his surprise, it was Max.

"Hold on, big fella; it's me." Max picked up speed with a quick waddle-like step. "What you think about the show? Pretty fucking fantastic. Your girl is something else, and boy, am I glad to see you home. Everybody is.

By the way, patrol caught those kids you told them about. You were right; they were up to no good. They had someone's Rolex, a diamond ring, a few hundred in cash, and now they all got criminal records, now. Stupid fuckers. They were over eighteen, so no skating there. You know we could pick up dem seventeens, but usually, unless it's bad shit, we give 'em a warning, ya know, scare the little turds." Max swayed back and forth as he spoke.

Babe was waiting for questions about the Commander, but he wasn't going to be the one to bring it up. They got to the door of the hotel. "Why are you out so late? Shouldn't you be home already?" Max mopped his forehead with a handkerchief from his pocket. "You heard about the Marine Commander that got himself killed?" Babe nodded. "You know him?"

"Yes." Babe nodded again, void of expression, like he was numb. "He tried to talk me out of separation; he said civilian life wasn't meant for everyone, basically telling me it wasn't for me. So far, I think it's been okay. I woulda never met my girl or my dog." He reluctantly gave a half-smile. Babe was cool as a cucumber; he had righted a wrong and didn't have the slightest regret. "Be careful out there, Detective; I'm getting some shut-eye. Work tomorrow, ya know? I'll be on the construction site in the morning."

"Well, welcome home Marine. I know one little Creole girl that missed the hell outta ya."

HOME AT LAST

*T*he apartment felt empty without Trinity or Gunner, but he needed sleep desperately. He quickly showered and tucked into bed. Usually, he'd hear her come in from Louie's, but his sleep was unusually sound, and the next thing he knew, he was waking for work with her curled into his body. He kissed her forehead. Sleepily, she snuggled closer. Managing to slip out unnoticed, Babe and Gunner took off for his apartment and a morning workout. The workout wasn't all he'd hoped for since he had to guard his injury, but it was a start. Easing under the shower flashed memories of the snake and Chop and the nightmare; a Twilight Zone experience, but it was now his reality. Any chance of creating an intimate mental encounter with Trinity was long gone. He'd have to tap the thought in real time.

Babe and Gunner started the short run to the construction site; the whole time, he let his mind drift to the unhappy memory of his abduction and the time away from his girl. Something was going to have to give. Maybe it was time they moved in together. The only way to make it right in his mind meant he'd pay to stay at her place. He figured he'd run to the jewelry shop on Royal at lunch and have them work their magic with his grandmother's ring. She had been a statuesque woman, not as tall as his mother, but not far off. Certainly, her hands were twice the size of tiny Trinity's. He wondered if the jeweler had the rubber-looking bands he'd seen so many men on the construction site wear.

His phone rang. "Vicarelli, "he answered with studdered breaths.

"This is Hurley. Have you given any thought to the meeting with Pierce?"

He stopped running for a second. "I've thought about it, and yeah, I'll meet with him, but it's not a commitment. I have something else I might want to do. It's not as glorious, but I'd need a unit of people special ops trained, probably some feds, which maybe your guy could assist, but I'm on my way to work. I'll call you later. Meet tomorrow evening or Sunday day or night. Later, dude."

Once on the construction site, it was easy to get into a rhythm. Babe went over the plans for the Conti job with Glenn, and it was pretty straightforward. He'd be minding the sheep, making sure everybody was pulling their weight and scheduling the subcontractors. The company had been in business for years, and while Glenn had been there five years, everyone who was anyone in the construction world knew him. "It is good to have you back, Vicarelli. You gave the family quite a scare. How's my Gunn?" He ruffled the fur.

Babe had been wanting to ask Glenn why he'd never mentioned being Bethany's fiancée. The opportunity hadn't come up as it was the barbeque night when Hell opened up with a crapton of serious threats leading to life-or-death situations. Babe leaned on the table to the side of Glenn's desk. "Why didn't you tell me you were engaged to Trinity's sister? Did you meet her before working here or after?"

Glenn rocked in his chair. "The how we met story is funny and different. I was working for a different construction company; oh, I knew of FQR&D. They had most of the French Quarter locked up, and I'd heard of the legendary Joe Gio, Joseph Giorlando. As a side note, I don't know if you've heard it called Ford Construction. The tail of the 'Q" broke off at the office. It never got fixed. Anyway, I went to my site super, I was assistant super, and asked for more money. He says, 'No can do,' but says Joe Gio was retiring. Maybe I might want to check it out, not that he wanted to lose me, but he understood I needed a raise." Babe intently listened while grabbing a cup of coffee.

"I go to one of their jobs in the Marigny after work, thinking the odds of catching the site super was probably nil, but I'd leave my number. Here's this sixty-something-year-old man, I'm guessing, sweeping the site. Me thinking it had to be the site grunt, ya know. I introduced myself and asked if I could leave a card for Mr. Giordano. He says, 'Ya got him, sonny.' I was shocked, but then this little sports car pulled up, and a cute dark-haired girl got out and ran up to him. She lays a big kiss on the cheek, and they talk. She was pretty and girlie. The site super introduced me to Bethany. Weird, right? He tells her I'm the guy replacing him when he retires. He blew me away; I was shocked." By this time, Babe is sitting in another chair, listening to a long, rambling answer Glenn could have answered in two words, not a diatribe. Babe nodded as he listened.

"He didn't know me from Adam, didn't know shit about me. She gets all squealy and hugs me. Okay, I was a bit freaked."

"I bet you were," he commented. *How does one say thanks I've heard all I need to hear without being rude? No, one just listens.*

"She says, 'Dad said if you had your replacement today, we all had to celebrate.' Then, to top it off, she says the dad will be happy to meet me and to see them at Irene's. By this time, my head was spinning. We hadn't talked but a minute. After the girl leaves, Joe says, 'Thanks, kid; I told Antoine I'd have everything set by today, which was weeks ago. You bailed me, and I gotta tell you, there will not be one day you regret working for Antoine. I hope you won't make a liar out of me. You gonna take the job? I said yes. I had no idea of pay when to start, or if I wanted to work for the Noelles," Glenn used air quotes when he mentioned Noelles. "So, the same damn day, I met her and got the job. We sat next to each other during dinner and talked, and as they say, the rest is history." *Glad the dissertation is over, but it answers my question.*

Babe needed to let his wandering mind take a rest. Who cares if he was into the family's questionable practices? It didn't matter. He still hadn't seen Antoine since the ordeal. Would their exchanges change? Would expectations be different? To stop the incessant postulating with his mind traveling at the speed of light, buzzing so much his mind was spinning, he asked Glenn if he wanted him to go to Conti and he'd retrieve Gunner when he returned. Glenn nodded with a wink. *Wink? What? A secret I don't know?*

Babe's phone rang. A smooth, velvet-like voice said, "Word has it, a serial killer murdered the Commander. I'd say it is an accurate statement; however, it is not the killer they think. Captain, you do have an intriguing skill set, I must say. I wish you had taken me up on my offer here in Cartagena. No hard feelings; I am confident we will encounter each other again." There was an eery silence in the background, not like the peaceful quiet he'd experienced during his stay. Maybe the lush surroundings softened the stillness, camouflaging a more sinister void in humanity.

"Who knows?" Babe was aloof. Hell, yes, they might meet each other again. He would go to the makeshift metal building and retrieve the abducted kids, come Hell or high water. Then, if Trinity wanted him to work the security gig, he would; if not, he wouldn't and spend his nights watching her do her thing at Louie's Tap. He pulled up to the Conti Street construction site. "This has been fun, but I gotta get to work. Ya know, keepin it real."

"Take care, Captain, and I'm impressed; it didn't take long to accomplish your goal."

"Hasta la vista."

The construction had not begun, only minor demolition. The centuries-old building had collapsed in places, and the plan was to excavate the ruins, secure the foundation, and maintain as much of the original building as possible. It was one of the issues with construction in the Quarter that many companies struggled with, but not FQR&D.

Regulations were such that contractors must protect as much of the antiquity as possible and all attempts made to replicate the old-world look. While Antoine had most of the city in his pocket, he would never allow for a modern metallic and glass edifice constructed by his company. His pedigree of generational French Quarter business owners ingrained a genuine attachment and love for French Quarter charm and finery.

Antoine Noelle was a complicated man of eccentricities and dichotomy. On the one hand, he was an astute businessman who participated in greasing the right palms to get what he wanted, yet he was a lover of stipulation and regulation. Babe had seen him somewhat in action, and the man behind the desk or on the other side of the phone seemed nothing like the man sitting at the end of the church pew or engaging with family, yet both fit him like a glove and wreaked of authenticity. What would Mr. Noelle think of a son-in-law interested in striking down child endangerment—interfering with other people's businesses? Would he strongly discourage his wild child from marrying such a thorn? Antoine knew the kind of man Babe was, passed no judgment so it seemed, but sabotaging another's livelihood, creating enemies, Antoine might frown upon such. The Marine felt a strong compulsion to end what he'd seen. It was as though there would be no turning a blind eye. His mission was always to protect the weak; those kids were merely an inventory, a commodity in the monster's hands. The thought of Jacob weighed heavy on his soul. *Yes, I have a heart; yes, I have a soul, fucking doctors.*

Babe's mind ticked over the thoughts as he wandered the soon-to-be construction site. A few men, obviously of Latin descent, nodded and smiled as they went about dismantling the wreckage. He wondered if they were here of their own volition or had someone imported them against their will. Were they working off a debt? After a thorough walk through the crumbling property, he left via the jewelry store on Royal Street.

Trinity rolled over, stretching the sleep from her body. A glow shone from her face, emanating rest, happy, and calm. Life looked like she remembered it and had longed for. Grabbing Babe's pillow, she hugged it, breathing deeply. He was home and had been in her bed, their bed. Tingles of excitement ran up her body—toes to head. *Wonder what he's doing?*

She knew Bethany and her mom were again in the throes of wedding decisions. While they had hired a planner, there was no way Mama Noelle was letting go of the power. She remembered the wedding to Joey. While he was a nice boy, he and Trinity were too young in her parent's eyes, and the wedding was like a practice run, lovely and pretty but without the sparkle of a Cinderella experience. It had been nice, but not a spectacle like what they were planning for Bethany, but then again, her sister had gone through all the proper channels.

When the time came for her and Babe to say 'I do,' it would be different. She didn't want a huge, flamboyant wedding but something significant to their relationship. It would be small, intimate with family and a few friends, and filled with joy. She felt the spark of true love when she looked at Babe. Trinity dressed and went to her mom's.

After circling the block a few times, there was nowhere to park. He'd have to bite the bullet and pay twenty dollars at a parking garage for a half-hour stop at the jewelry store. The truck was getting to be too much hassle. Perhaps a Harley might be a better option in the Quarter. It would have to be big; otherwise, he'd look like a clown in one of those trick circus cars.

Behind the glass case in the back was an older gentleman, maybe one might say archaic; nonetheless, if anyone could help him, it'd be that guy. "Welcome. How can I be of assistance?" Babe showed him the ring. Quickly, the man pulled out his loupe, studying the ring. "Young man, this is a beautiful work of craftsmanship. You don't see this kind of workmanship anymore, and the stones, ah, they are magnificent. How can I help?"

"I'd like to get this sized for my girlfriend. She's a petite woman. The ring was my grandmother's; she was a statuesque person." The jeweler shook his head.

"You can only size it smaller so much with this design, and take it from me; you won't find anything this quality. Very few of us are left; I've been in the business since I was a boy, following in my father and grandfather's shoes. Years ago, our lapidarist, those who actually cut stones, used to cut them differently. While many people prefer the newer cuts, saying the stone becomes more brilliant, I am of a different opinion, but I'm an old man." The man sucked in his mouth, lips wide and teeth clenched, almost with a look of constipation. "I'd hate to ruin this ring. It is magnificent. For perfection, I would need to remake it properly, which might take some time." He kissed the tips of his fingers with a flick and winked. "Are you in a hurry?" Babe responded he wasn't and asked if he had rubber wedding bands. "You must work with your hands. I have a few, but your fingers are big. Let's see what I have?" Talking to himself, he opened a drawer and pulled out a box. He dug around for a few minutes, then his eyebrows arched up into peaks, and he exclaimed, "Try this on." Babe smiled; it fit perfectly, and the ring was exactly what he wanted—black.

"Sold. Do you have any of those in tiny sizes?" The man rolled his eyes. "While I wait for the diamond engagement ring." The man nodded.

"I have one size four. It's pink, not black. The silicone bands are all the rave and, in my opinion, trash, but it's what you young people want, so I say, okay, I'll carry some. You want the pink one?" Babe smiled.

"Yes, sir. How much do I need to pay you for the sizing of the diamond ring?"

After a half-hour, Babe walked out satisfied. The man said he wouldn't do it if it might ruin the ring or, with Babe's permission, make one similar using the stones, but it would be expensive. They agreed; he shoved the pink band in his pocket to give Trinity later, got his truck, and headed to the job site.

The ring was bothersome at first, but this might keep unwanted advances. He and Glenn looked over the plans. "What gives with the band, Vicarelli? Did Trinity give you a Promise ring?" Babe laughed.

"I was hoping it might quell unwanted advances," he raised his eyebrows with a smirk. "I got one for her too." A lump developed in his throat. *Bottled emotion over a fucking ring?*

"Don't be surprised if it increases the flirting. Ya know, forbidden fruit?" He smiled. "I didn't know y'all were that serious." Glenn wasn't prying out of gossip; he wanted to know. Babe shrugged a shoulder but slung a half-smile. He figured the writing was on his face, but there were so many unknowns—like the future, where he'd be, and what she would be willing to put up with. Would she see his way in wanting to retrieve the kids in Cartagena? "Word of warning, friend, Antoine's gonna have a ton of questions; prepare yourself when you ask for her hand." *Ask for her hand. Is that still a thing?*

Louie's was quiet, with only a few people sitting at the bar. He knew to give it an hour or two, and the crowds would emerge and pack it out. Trinity was engrossed in working on a blender and didn't see him come in, but when Gunner ran around the bar, she startled with a slight jump and turned to see Babe at the bar. She grabbed a chew toy from under the bar and tossed it as she rounded the bar. Gunner took chase, allowing space next to Babe. "Hi." She pecked him, "How was work?" Immediately, she grabbed his hand, "What is on your finger?"

"Give me your hand." He put the bright pink ring on her finger. "This is yours. I know they aren't the real thing, but until then, it'll keep interested parties at bay, maybe. At least I'm staking my claim when I'm not here." She threw her arms around him and kept looking at it.

"This is perfect for being at the bar with my hands in water all the time; I love it. So, what does this mean?" She looked at him with a cocked brow.

"It means you're mine, and I'm yours. Good enough for now?"

She smiled with a light laugh, "Yes, sir." He kissed her.

"Gunner and I are heading to the boys. I'll see you later tonight." She seemed enthusiastic and kept looking at her finger. She blew him a kiss as he and Gunner walked out of Louie's.

On his way to Chestnut, his phone rang. "Vicarelli."

"Thanks for my ring. I love it." It warmed his heart to hear her squeal with excitement.

"I'm glad." After an I love you they disconnected.

His phone rang again, "Again?"

"Hello? Captain Vicarelli?" The voice asked with a quiver.

"This is Vicarelli."

"I wanted to call you, sir. I know you wanted to surprise the Commander, and I hate to say this, but no need to come here. He passed." It was Daniel. He wanted to say, 'No, he didn't pass; I killed the fucker,' but thanked him for the heads up. "Can we still go for a drink sometime?"

Babe chuckled. "If you're free tonight, how 'bout I buy you a beer at Louie's Tap? I'll meet you at twenty-thirty?"

"Yes, sir. Twenty-thirty, it is."

By this time, he pulled into the driveway at Chestnut. Gunner lunged out of the truck and ran to the gate. Once inside, he was all over the boys. "I get here in time for dinner?"

Ruthie had her back to him. "Just." Her voice sounded different. Then she sniffled.

"Are you sick?" She shook her head no, and then he saw her shoulders shudder. He turned her to him. She was crying. "You okay?" She shook her head. "What's wrong? The boys—"

She interjected, "Clive got jumped and beaten bad. Real bad."

Babe's jaw jutted forward. "Who and where?"

"What's done is done." She wiped her nose. She looked weak and, for the first time, perhaps her age. Her son's beating crushed her spirit.

"No, ma'am. Where did it happen, and did he know the people?" Babe put his arm around her shoulder. "When did this happen, Ruthie?"

She explained getting into his truck a few nights before; three hoodlums tried to jack his vehicle. Rather than handing it over, he fought them, and they beat him nearly to death. He asked where Clive was, and she answered he was in the city hospital. He'd been there for two days since the night of the incident; lucky, a neighbor saw him lying in the street. Babe wanted the room number so he could pay a visit, then asked if the thugs had his truck. To her knowledge, she said they did.

"What's done, sir, is done. His insurance will handle things. Don't you go worrying none. You got enough with your own problems." During the conversation, she had plated the food. "Call on up to the boys, if you will." There were too many things simultaneously needing his attention. Babe wanted to talk to Jacob, Clive, and then he needed to meet Daniel at Louie's.

The Jacob Q&A would take hours, and he could see Clive after a drink with Daniel. It was always good to have someone on the inside, and in Daniel's position, Babe hoped to open some doors or answer some of the questions he still had. Was anyone else connected to Javier's world, or was the Commander a lone rogue wolf dipping his toe into the massive sea of money?

A CONFEDERACY OF BED FELLOWS

*H*eading down St. Charles Avenue toward the Quarter, he observed the diverse gathering of people waiting for the street car. It was a mixture of older folks, the usual business passengers, and teens looking like they were up to no good. What had happened to the city? It had always been rife with colorful elements or what one might deem sleazy or immoral, but the likes of the girls dancing on the poles was a different ambiance to those living in the grandeur of mansions along the avenue. His grandfather would say the owners had an air of old money. It used to make Babe chuckle to himself. The stately old Norwegian had accrued enough wealth for several lifetimes. He missed the old guy, and whenever he let his mind wander to their conversations, it felt like a gaping hole formed in his heart, and a heaviness weighed on his soul.

Trinity had often mentioned he should park in the hotel garage rather than on the street. Still, he always seemed to luck out and find a big enough parking spot—sometimes on the outskirts of the Quarter, but all within easy walking distance. Tonight would be different; he would park at the Hotel Noelle; time was a factor.

Babe took his seat at the end of the bar, but Trinity was nowhere in sight. *Curious.* Finn poured his Glenlivet and whispered to the big man, "She's in the—" and nodded his head with raised eyebrows toward the restrooms. It seemed an age before she came to the bar. His girl looked sick; she'd lost the glimmer in her eyes, and the smile seemed forced.

He beckoned with his finger. Trinity responded, but not with the usual playful fluttering of her lashes and dimpled smile. "Hey, you," she said, trying her best to look well.

"Finn's poured my drink, and I don't need to eat. I had—" With that, she sprinted to the restroom.

Babe glanced at Finn as he made his way to the facilities. Finn shrugged a shoulder, "She's been like that all night. Can't talk about food, or she ralphs. She's not even interested in dancing."

"Since she came on this afternoon?"

"Yup. Your girl is sick as a dog. She took something and said she'd be fine in a little bit for the show." Finn waggled his eyebrows.

"It's almost," he paused, "twen—um, eight-thirty, and she's been like this since coming in?"

Standing outside the door to the women's room, he cracked the door. "Trinity, are you okay?" He heard her wretch again. "Coming in, " he announced in case other women were in the room. No one responded or commented, so he entered. He dampened a paper towel and handed it to her. "You eat something bad?" Another wave of puke flooded the toilet. "Maybe you should go home." She wiped her mouth and stood straight, shaking her head.

"I took some Emetrol; it should start working soon. It's a miracle in a bottle." She eeked out a smile. She dug in her pocket and pulled out a peppermint. "This will help too." She put her arms around his waist. "Sorry. I take it all is good with you." He nodded, but she could see the concern on her big guy's face. "Babe, I'm okay."

Once settled, they walked out into the barroom. Babe told her about Daniel coming to Louie's later. "It's always good to have a connection like

Daniel. I'm not sure what his title is, but he seems someone low enough on the totem pole not to be a threat yet high enough to know the scuttlebutt." He kissed the top of her head. She looked beautiful; she'd pulled her hair up with a few escaped tendrils. Having her hair away from her face accentuated how gorgeous she was—her features were so tiny and perfect.

Moments after taking his seat, Daniel entered. Babe was easy to spot; he grabbed the stool beside the big guy. "Glad you made it, Daniel."

"Are you kidding? It'll be the highlight of my week—home to work and nothing in between. This thing," he knocked on his prosthetic leg, "isn't a chick magnet."

Trinity made her way to the end of the bar, where Babe introduced her to Daniel Collins. "Welcome to Louie's. You served with Vic? I bet you have secrets about the big guy I'd be willing to pay money for." She rendered a throaty laugh. "Seriously, what ya havin', Marine?"

Trey had five files opened in front of him. He read over them carefully, then looked up at Max.

"What's that look about, Trey? Something red hot in one of them file folders you got?" He took a draw on a Diet Coke. Waiting for an answer. Like usual, Trey noodled his idea before posing the question, and to Max, it was a most annoying habit, almost as irritating as the clickety-click pen.

"I have four victims with their necks snapped. The dumpster guy had broken hands, an arm, one of his legs, and his neck. Coincidence? I think we have a serial killer out there. It takes someone with the aptitude and training to snap a neck." Their eyes met. "Then, there was the guy tryin' to hose his girlfriend's kid, sliced across his throat almost ear to ear." The pen action began, and Trey was on a roll. "Think about it." He put one finger up, "The guy in the doorway around the time of the spring breakers; two, the dumpster dude from the job site; three, and four, the kidnappers—"

Max interjected, "No, she didn't have a broken neck; I remember she had a crushed skull; besides, that was a vehicular accident. Those weirdos were stoned and driving like lunatics. The way I see it, if we do have a serial killer, he's taking out the trash. Good riddance."

Trey shook his head. Murder was murder; nothing righteous about it. To Max's point, the killer targeted scum, not any innocents. 'Someone trained' darted through his mind, and the face repeatedly popping up was Babe. As much as he liked the guy, he had felt an ominous vibe from him on a few occasions. No doubt he could easily take out any of the victims. "Max, like it or not, we have to interview Babe."

"Think about it, Studly; most of those crimes occurred when he was with us. Think of it logically—" he was resting on his elbows with his hands held out.

"I am. I don't like it any more than you do. I've considered that Babe was with us and the accident he called in. Now, if he'd done the deed, do you think he woulda hung around? See the catch, he's smart, and yes, he well may have called it in and been the doer." They argued the situation; finally, Max agreed they'd talk to him and put feelers out. They headed out of the precinct to Louie's. It was well past eight, and he'd told Steph he'd be home no later than seven. He was already gonna be in the dog house; a few more minutes wouldn't make a difference.

They heard the music from a block away, and like most nights since the new bartender's show, they'd drawn a hefty crowd. Weaving through the hoard of customers was a feat in itself. Babe looked over Daniel's head and saw them approaching. He slung a one-sided smile in their direction. He cupped his hand to his comrade's ear, who was sitting beside him, obviously a Marine. Daniel turned his head and nodded to the detectives. They finally made it to them. Trinity saw the two and pointed to her waist. They nodded, and she brought a Diet Coke and soda with lime. The music quieted for a brief minute. "Detectives, this is Daniel Collins. We served for a time together."

The Marine returned the nod with a downcast feeling to his smile. "Captain Vicarelli is the real deal, gentlemen." He knocked on his left leg. "Lost it, but he carried me and saved my life. He never let us down, never. First in and last out." The thought wrenched Trey's heart. How could he think Babe was behind the murders? Admittedly, anything they had was circumstantial at best, and one could easily argue he was in the wrong place at the right time. He tended to the kidnap victims until help arrived, and the same thing happened regarding the young man who took a bullet on the sidewalk behind him. The victim reported how the big man took over until the EMTs showed up. Trey already knew because he had beaten the EMTs to the scene. He rested on the bar, drank the soda and lime, and watched the show. The serial killer possibility weighed heavy on his mind. He didn't want it to be true, but the way things lined up waved a red flag.

A lull broke for a second. Babe leaned over to Trey, "Y'all in the thick of it right now? Something going on around here?"

Trey smiled, "Something like that. Hey, we might need your help. Can you come to the station tomorrow?"

"Sure, but I don't get off until seventeen, um, five. I have something I have to do with one of the boys. Maybe I'll stop in around noon." Trinity captured his attention, and he looked away from Trey for a minute. "Fucking amazing." Babe returned his attention to Trey. "Noon?" The detective pointed at him and winked, confirming the appointment. The next step was up to Trey and Max to find a way into the big man's head. They left shortly after draining their glasses.

"I see you have a wedding ring," Daniel commented. "Married, kids?" He tilted his head to the side with a smile. "I knew you'd find your special someone. The scuttlebutt was, uh, never mind. Happy for you." Daniel's comment piqued Babe's curiosity; he couldn't imagine people gossiping about him. "Boys? How old?"

Babe cleared his throat and chuckled softly. "Not married and no kids. The band is a barrier to unwanted advances. I got her one, too," and he directed his gaze at Trinity. "The kids are a long story, but they're basically street kids that I've adopted, not legally, but getting them off the street and in school." Daniel proceeded to ask more questions; it was the time of night when he wanted to head to Trinity's. "It's been good catching up, but I gotta call it a night. I have to be on the job site early." They touched fists, and Babe beckoned Trinity. She came around the bar and told him she'd see him at home, which meant her place.

Daniel put his hand on Babe's shoulder, "Hey, if your lady knows anyone who may be interested in a mangled Marine, let me know. My nights get lonely; you get what I mean."

Walking to Trinity's, he remembered wanting to talk to Clive. Maybe Trey and Max might have a contact or information; no, first, he'd try on his own. Babe wondered what Trey and Max could want from him; the curiosity wasn't anything to keep him up, though. Sleep fell upon him fast; the next thing he knew, it was three in the morning, and he woke to the sound of Trinity vomiting. He wet a washcloth and put it on her neck. "You need to see a doctor. Are you drinking enough fluids? FYI, vomiting can dehydrate you. I'm serious; you really need to see a quack and stay home."

She knew there was no reason to see a doctor and had a reasonably good idea what the problem could be, but thought for another time and a whole different conversation. They fell asleep, their bodies conforming to each other. Trinity fit perfectly into the curve of his body—his shoulders and head poking out along with his calves and feet. She curled in a tiny ball against his body.

The morning routine went like clockwork, and on his run to the construction site, he received a call from Antoine. He stopped running, a bit exasperated at the interruption, "Yes, sir."

"What are you going to the P.D. for?" *How the fuck does he know?* "You know you gotta watch every word you say. Do you want my attorney with you?"

"Thanks for the offer, but I'm an attorney; besides, they want help with something. Nothing to worry about, sir." They hung up, and he continued onto the site. Thoughts zoomed through his mind during the run to work. It was bothersome Antoine knew about the NOPD thing. He liked privacy and felt it was fast disappearing. Were Trey and Max a part of the Noelle enterprise? He never got the feeling of them as crooked cops, but he let his mind wander. Somewhere along the way, Babe remembered a reference to after his abduction and Trey and Max attending to the incident and the presence of Antoine. He weighed the thought; of course, her father would go to the scene. The hotel was blocks away, and it was his baby girl, but it still didn't pacify the angst. Babe didn't want Antoine into all his business, but then again, he had opened the door when calling him for Trinity's protection. Relationships were something he never wanted; they did nothing but complicate things, and his life recently had been one mess after another. In the innermost part of his being, Babe loved Trinity, but a steady girlfriend, soon-to-be wife, wasn't part of the equation for him. Their relationship created too much havoc and discomfort.

While all these scrambled ideas bounced around, he felt distracted and as though any mojo had flown in the wind. During times apart, his every thought was of getting back to her. Everything about life flashed to her face. Perhaps he needed to derail the rampage of ideas and focus on one thing at a time.

He looked at Gunner, "Things are way fucked up, my friend. While Deary ended up being a piece of shit, he was right about one thing— civilian life was not for me. Now, Gunn, I'm in a FUBAR world and don't like it." Gunn took off as they neared the construction site and ran up the stairs into the office. Glenn poked his head out, looking for Babe.

As he punched the time clock, he asked Glenn, "Does it ever bother you that Bethany's dad seems to know all your business?"

Glenn's eyebrows raised in curiosity, "He doesn't, or I'm not aware he does. It's not like I have anything to hide, but he's never once asked me anything. Why is he getting too inquisitive about your relationship with Trinity? Remember I asked you if he was okay with y'all being together, and at the time, you seemed to think it was a non-issue. Also, man, Trinity has given him way harder of a time than Bethany."

Babe shrugged his shoulder, "Maybe my background has him squirrely or spooked. I'm leaving for lunch and might be back a little later than an hour. Any issue?"

"Nope. Make sure to stop in on the other project while you're out." Glenn started to look over a spreadsheet and then paused, raised his head, and zeroed in on the big guy's face with a set and intense look. "Vic, everything okay with you, man?" He shook his head and left the trailer, getting to the task where he had left off the day before.

Noon came faster than he would have liked, and he headed to the police department. Nothing in his life felt right. Uncertainty was like a blanket of heaviness in his every move, the traps of being a civilian. The way to the precinct was about a fifteen-minute walk; thoughts of a motorcycle crossed his mind again. Once inside, a uniformed officer led him to Trey and Max.

"What's up, Babe? Follow me." Trey asked, and the detectives led him to a conference room. Each had a few files in their arm. Everyone grabbed a seat. Trey was the token spokesperson he gathered because the young detective was the first to speak. "Wanted to pick your brain." Babe listened. "There have been a few unusual murders in the French Quarter over the past several months. It's not the usual drug deal gone bad or lover's triangle murder of passion. No, these seem purposeful, for lack of a better word. What we need your help with: wait, let me clarify. These victims have had their necks broken. My question to you is, who might be trained to kill in such a way?" Trey had the blank pad in front of him with his clickety pen.

Babe placed his hands flat on the table and answered with a sober tone, "I can; it's not too terribly hard. It's about the right amount of torque and angle sometimes, but almost any trained person in the military could undoubtedly do the deed. But for proficiency, it'd be someone with more extensive training, hand-to-hand kinda stuff. I'd speculate most of your martial arts instructors would be capable, maybe MMA fighters; I don't know if y'all have any trainers that come to mind in New Orleans. I don't work out at a gym, and I'm not sure what or who around here is into survival training or combat. Also, another thought: check out those whacked end-of-times militia groups."

Babe leaned forward on his elbows as though getting engrossed in the conversation. He knew damn well why they brought him in, and with due reason.

"Another thing to look at, not telling you your business, but if it were me, I'd look into the victims; is there a pattern there? Mainly guys, not that I don't like shooting the shit with you, but why are you asking me? Is it because I got so interested in the college kid situation? Nothing personal, but at this time, I have no desire to join law enforcement. Something I am interested in, and maybe y'all could direct me. What department is dealing with all the street kid abductions? I've rescued three so far but know of more."

At the same time, Trey and Max were thrown off focus and became intrigued with the big man's story. Their original hypothesis of Babe being a serial killer had lost momentum, and he'd provided a tenable list of possibilities, and it wasn't like he rehearsed. They could tell Babe was searching for viable options to help. They had been on the wrong path in their thinking; he was merely low-hanging fruit. And to Max's point, whoever was committing the murders was eliminating the trash off the streets and doing the cops a favor. After a few niceties, Babe headed to the other construction site. It was mostly a demo deal, and from what he could tell, the guys knew what they were doing.

THE DEEPER
IT GETS

*A*t first, working for Glenn felt fulfilling enough and was a basic job. Since all the scandal and Antoine's outspoken concerns, it seemed like Glenn assigned jobs anyone could do—like a fucking stooge position. The more time pressed on, the more he accepted civilian life was not for him.

Babe's phone buzzed, "Heya, Babe, we never answered your question regarding the missing kids. I have a friend with Homeland named Bryan Bell; give him a shout. Sending his contact info to you, but I'll give him a heads-up to expect your call. You'd make a good fed. In the funnies." Max disconnected and shot him the contact information.

Now, he had another something to process. He was struggling with spinning all the plates. It seemed like the story of the abducted kids might let people get too close to him. This is not what he wanted. Chop was easy to blame, but truthfully, it all started with his Trinity fascination. Why did he think he could have a life like everyone else? He was different than most. He didn't want trouble, but it seemed to follow him from every direction.

Babe figured he'd make the call the following day, giving Max a chance to hear from his friend. As he turned onto the nearly finished site, his phone buzzed. He didn't recognize the number. "Vicarelli."

"Good afternoon, sir. This is Bryan Bell. Max told me you'd be calling and gave me the broad brush impression he gleaned from you. I want to meet with you; I understand time is a factor."

"Affirmative, sir."

"Can we meet around six tonight? From what I've understood, the only help I can give you is to turn you onto a friend of mine; rescuing trafficked people, especially kids, is his mission." *And yet another person in the debacle.* "There are dozens of organizations, but this guy is the real deal. He's had training like you; I think he was a SEAL. Am I correct in saying you were a Raider?"

"Where to meet?" Babe inquired.

"Jackson Square. It'll be quick. I'm hooking you up with this guy, like the middleman."

"Can do, sir. Eighteen hundred or thereabout?" The conversation ended, and Babe turned his entire focus to the job.

Glenn was going through looking for any blemishes. He gave Babe a roll of blue tape. Finding an irregularity was something he could do well. His internal radar picked up on any discrepancies or things out of place and not squared. He had placed three tape markers for every one Glenn set. He definitely had a discerning eye. "Vic, you done this before?"

"No, sir, but I'm detail-oriented. One has to be, or you risk getting killed and those around you—trip wires, IEDs, glare from a sniper rifle, snaps in branches, you get the drift." Babe placed two more markers. "Demo guys seem to know what they're doing on Conti. They appear very particular in their dismantling." They finished the blue tape adventure.

The two men jumped in Glenn's Jeep for a quick stop at the demolition. They walked through some rubble; Babe leaned over and pulled a strand of beads from under a rock. One of the workmen smiled, so he tossed the plastic treasure to him. "Well spotted," Glenn chuckled. "You're like a good hunting dog, an invaluable asset."

"Where do you find good labor or skilled labor?" Babe observed the care one of the men had taken in removing a long piece of molding.

Glenn put his finger up to say in a minute. He spoke fluent Spanish to the man who had been so careful with the molding. The conversation continued for about five minutes, then Glenn returned to Babe.

"Handy to know the language, I'm guessing." Glenn laughed, saying his grandmother was from Spain, and while some of her words didn't translate the same as Mexican Spanish, it was close enough.

They walked to the car. Glenn answered Babe's question about hiring a workforce. FQR&D had a massive list of suppliers and tradespeople, but if they ran short of a gofer, they could find people at Home Depot, but it wasn't the norm. They wanted to know the people who worked on their projects.

"Wanna grab a beer?" Glenn asked as they were leaving for the day.

"Can't today, but maybe next time." Babe was most interested in talking to Bryan Bell's contact, but he still didn't like the idea of too many people being in the mix. He'd have to use generalities, not specifics.

Once again, he parked at Hotel Noelle and stopped in quickly to touch base with Trinity. He gave her the skinny on the conversation with Trey and Max. She raised an eyebrow. He knew what was going through her head, and she'd be right. He told her about Max's referral regarding the child abduction. She seemed as interested as he was, which gave him the impression any involvement he had may not be a sticking point with her, but there was no point in bringing it up yet. She poured him a short Glenlivet, which he swallowed in one gulp. Babe gave her a quick kiss and headed out to Jackson Square.

Two men sat on a bench between the square and the Cathedral. He bet the thin one was near fifty, if not early fifties, with dark coffee-colored skin and more pepper than salt in his hair. He looked like a Bryan, a fed—groomed but not making a fashion statement. The other man looked like a wrestler, broad-chested and meaty, which reminded him of his old wrestling coach. Coach Kennedy had always maintained his fitness and was a powerhouse.

The other man waiting was physically fit with a youthful look to his face, Babe speculated the man was near his age, late thirties; he looked like someone from special ops.

Both men stood as he walked up to greet them. The thin older man introduced himself, "Max described you to a tee, Captain Vicarelli, right?" Babe gave a half-smile.

"Yes, sir, Vic is fine," he glanced back and forth between them.

"Well, Vic, I'm Bryan, and this is Jarvis. The two men shook hands. Now that y'all have met, I must be heading home. Thank you both for making time." *Odd*.

The conversation started with Jarvis asking Babe what he knew about human trafficking. Like in CliffsNotes, Babe gave the short version of the Chop story, catching him loading the copter, all the way through the cartel experience, and picking up Jacob. He added, while not legally, he more or less adopted the two boys Chop tried to abduct, as well as young Jacob. The man listened intently.

"Then, you know how bad it is and what happens to these kids. What is it you want to do about it?" Jarvis leaned forward, elbows on his thighs. "Vic, I'm committed to the plight, or should I say fight. It gets repulsive. I've had to work in conjunction with local authorities, and you never know who you can trust. The people you have to associate with are pedophiles, traffickers, and scum; you have to get down and dirty with them. Is that what you're looking to do? Cause brotha, it will consume your life." The whole time he spoke, he looked Babe directly in the eyes. He had a nice manner of speaking, rather soft-spoken, but no doubt he could take care of business.

Babe held his thought, trying to express his interest without sounding self-indulgent or ignorant. "The kid I told you about in the warehouse was dirty and hungry. From the driver's questions, more kids or people were in the makeshift warehouse. It literally was pieces of sheet metal positioned almost like a house of cards. I want to get them all but don't know how many or what to do with them once I'm there. Do I rent a bus, if they even have one, or some delivery truck? I don't know if there are four or forty."

The man, Jarvis, reclined on the seat of the bench. "You're right; time is precious. Can you find out more from the boy you have? Also, know it may be completely different, and they may have changed locations—"

Babe interrupted, "I'd do it myself, but I am clueless about what to do. Would you be willing to go with me? I think I could get someone I served with for a time to assist, or do you take the information and go for it? You'd never see it if you didn't know where this place was. They have it camouflaged well."

"Where?" Jarvis asked.

"Cartagena."

"Of course it is," he exclaimed sarcastically. "There are cruise ships that specifically go there strictly for pedo parties. They pay big bucks and choose the kids they want. Man, it's vile, and those are the people you have to deal with for them to consider you legit. Sorry, but you wreak of Marine, padna. Talk to your boy; this is my number," he wrote on the back of a business card from some beauty salon. Babe examined the card. "Oh, we got more than our share in the States. Many of the massage parlors or salons offering massage are run by scuz that are making these people pay off their debt. Which, by the way, never gets paid off. Life-long slavery. You got the stomach for it?" Jarvis ran his hand down his face. "I'm not gonna lie; it's grim. You have to go in knowing you won't be able to save them all; you can hope, but you have to understand the odds are greatly against you."

"I don't know." Babe's forehead creased as he shook his head. "I have no idea other than I'm disgusted. I want to get the kids from the warehouse, and then I'll consider more. My lady has to be good with it. She knows my feelings on the knowledge I have, but some of this other stuff, I don't know." Babe gave Jarvis his phone number. "We'll meet again, but I want to act on this soon."

Jarvis got up, faced Babe, shook hands, and said he'd be in touch. That was that. Babe didn't feel any more informed on the hows, but he also felt Jarvis was legit and would hear from him soon. He walked to Louie's, spent a moment with Trinity, and then said, "I'm off to the boys. I want to have a heart-to-heart with Jacob. If I don't make it back here, I'll be at your place when you get off."

Instead of going straight to Chestnut, he veered and went to University Hospital. It had been a hot minute since he was last there. His mind rolled back in time. On one of his leaves, he'd returned to New Orleans during Mardi Gras, one of his least favorite festivities; not saying he liked any in particular. Hurley had come to town and wanted to see the decadence for himself. They walked down Bourbon Street amidst the sea of people; a girl on a balcony called to Hurley something about beads. The drunk beside them shouted to show her tits, and she raised her shirt. He chucked a strand of beads to the girl. The chick's husband or boyfriend got pissed and threw something at the guy splitting his head. Hurley caught him as he tumbled backward.

They hailed a cab a few blocks over and took the drunk to University Hospital. Being Carnival time, it was a zoo, but Babe quickly realized no matter when or what time of year, the place was crazytown. People hustled at a clipping speed from point A to point B, constantly calling out commands or orders. A constant buzz of conversation, announcements over the PA system, and wailing created enough noise to initiate a heightened alert, similar to a warzone.

An elevator opened just as he got to it, and a crowd of people flooded out into the hallway. He quickly jumped in and went to Clive's room, which he shared with another young man. Ruthie was right; the thugs had beaten him to a pulp. Clive heard Babe enter and opened the one eye he could; the other was more at half-mast. "Good evening, Clive. Your mother told me about what happened. Did you know the guys or recognize them?" Clive nodded. "Have you reported it to the police?" He shook his head no.

"Why not? At least you might get your vehicle back."

"No, man, that's not how it rolls. 'Sides, it's probably been to some chop shop or torched in the east. My momma told me you was all badass, but brotha, I have similar skills to you, an' I shoulda never taken on the three of them. Lesson learned." He coughed slightly and grabbed his abdomen.

Babe grabbed a pillow from the closet. "Brace with this and try to cough harder. I'm surprised no one told you to splint." The big man towered over the bed. "Tell me a little something about these thugs."

Clive started to speak but coughed again, this time bracing with the pillow. "Naw, man, really." Babe cocked his head; he wasn't taking no for an answer. "One's named T-Train, and he lives on Toledano by South Prieur. The dude's a big sucker, not as large as you, but bigger than me, and has a full grill. I played in a card game a few weeks ago; he lost, and I made out flush. I guess it was retribution. Not playin' cards no more." He smiled the best he could. He had stitches in four spots on his face, one eye swollen nearly shut, a casted arm, and from the pain when he coughed, Babe suspected some broken ribs—it wouldn't be a surprise if he had some internal organ damage.

"Brotha, you get better. Your mother is worried. I know a few men I served with who are nasty. We may visit ya boy, T-Train, and I hope the other two jokers are with him. Say nothing to your mother. We straight?" Clive nodded.

Once out the door, he realized he had no intention of getting anyone else involved, loose ends and all. Suddenly, it dawned on him he was opening himself to other people, making him vulnerable as a kitten. Involving other people in his life was going to have to change. He wasn't and never had been a people person; it only led to disappointment referencing Deary. It had to be Trinity's influence, and if she wanted to be the life of the party or a social butterfly, that was fine. He'd sit on the sidelines and watch, making sure she was okay.

Babe pulled out into traffic headed toward Chestnut. Time being of the essence, he had to talk to Jacob alone for any details the boy could recall. He knew the story with Chris and Reg. The thought of the two boys made him question if life on the street had presented any attacks other than the one abduction, which was horrible in itself. Perhaps they'd learn not to do anybody else's drugs, or it was enough to convince them not to use drugs, even if it was only marijuana.

He pulled into the driveway and could smell a hint of the aroma from the evening's dinner, which was probably gone by then, merely the lingering empty promise of a tasty meal. The door sprung open, and Ruthie was standing with an ear-to-ear grin. "I had a feeling you'd be here for dinner, so I saved you a plate. Hungry?"

She walked in step with him. "Yes, ma'am. Where's Jacob? I need to see him."

"Doing his homework in the dining room. They used to do it in their bedrooms, but I caught them one too many times with the TV playing. Now I ask you, how can anyone learn anything with those ridiculous shows blaring in the background? I fixed the problem. Jacob should be near done. Sit, and I'll bring you a plate." He found it surprising three boys their ages sat quietly engrossed in schoolwork.

Chris glanced up. "I was hoping you would stop by tonight. I have a question for you." Babe sat with a slight smirk. He was glad to see them, too.

"So what's your question, little man?" Chris raised an eyebrow, nodding to the other two. "Maybe for a few minutes after I finish my food." He told Jacob they needed to talk, and the other two boys started making noise, taunting him like he was in trouble with Babe. "You did nothing wrong. Relax." The boys returned to their studies, glancing at the big man every few minutes.

"When you gonna stay here for the night?" Reg asked.

"Sunday," he responded off the cuff, hoping Trinity would be inclined. Babe finished his meal and brought the dishes into the kitchen to clean. Ruthie snatched them from him.

"It's getting late; hurry your talk with Jacob; he needs a full night's sleep." He wanted to say 'yes, Staff Sergeant,' but nodded instead. As he started to enter the dining room, Chris ran to him, grabbed his arm, and pulled him into the laundry room.

Babe became concerned, "What's up, Chris?"

In a hushed voice, he whispered, "Can you get me some condoms?" *Wow, what the fuck?* "I been pulling out, but I know girls who's gotten preggo with the baby cu—"

He had to think on his feet. If he said yes, he would be condoning the behavior, but if Chris was already tapping the fountain, then saying no would be irresponsible. Interrupting, he said, "Yeah, but no more sex until I get them, okay?" He agreed and left the room, running up the stairs. He heard Ruthie clear her throat, and the thunderous race up the stairs came to a halt. Odds were he was calling the girl with the info. Babe had to remind himself Chris was a sixteen-year-old street kid and had probably knocked boots plenty of times.

He returned to the dining room. "Reg, anything going on in your life you might want to discuss?" Babe sat across from Jacob.

"Nope, I mean, no, sir. The bully kid who stole my bike has treated me like one of the popular kids since we went and got it."

"Way to go," and he high-fived Reg as the boy started for the stairs. Babe waited until he heard Reg on the stairs. "Jacob, I have to ask you some questions that might make you feel uncomfortable, but it's things I need to know." The boy nodded. "How long were you in the metal warehouse?"

"Not sure, maybe three weeks." He sat with a stoic face. Babe knew it had to be hard to talk about.

"How many people would you say were in there with you, and were they little or around your age?"

"I know exactly how many because the head man counted us off when he handed out bottles of water. There were thirty-one; now I guess there's thirty. Unless—" he became silent. Babe felt guilty; it was almost like he was torturing the kid. He nodded at Jacob like saying, keep going. Jacob completed the thought, "The cruise ship was there. He'd take some of us, make us wear different clothes, and then bring us to the ship in a boat." Babe wanted to ask if he'd been on the boat but didn't; it might be too painful. "Most of the kids were ten to fourteen, but there were grownup ladies and a couple of younger kids, like five, I guess. They'd take some away every few days and bring new ones to fill the empty space. We had barely enough room to lie down, but mostly we sat. It was fuckin' hot as hell. I felt like I was in Hell. Many days, I wished I was never born and hoped the men would give me the shots like they did the women. It'd make them sleep, not enough to OD but man, they were fucked up. When they'd come down, they would try to scream. Dude, it was a nightmare. I thought sleeping behind the French Market was horrible, but the warehouse was way worse. Trust me." He paused, scrunching his nose like he'd smelled something awful. "There was a bucket everyone would shit in, but they pissed in the corners or right where they were. It was only when we'd go on the ship that we got to take a shower and use a toilet."

The question was answered, yes, he'd been to the party cruise and raped. He'd get the boy help. "Would you like to talk with someone about the experience?"

"You mean a fucking shrink? I've heard about them." He seemed aggravated and almost insulted.

Babe jumped in quickly, "I had to talk to a psychologist when I was your age and then again when I was leaving the Corps. I still talk to him now and then." Babe looked into Jacob's eyes, trying to say it would get better.

"Why'd you go when you were my age?" Babe had captured his attention.

"My father was an alcoholic and would beat my mother and me, and one day, I had enough and hit him over and over again with a kitchen chair until his shoulder broke and the chair was in a thousand pieces. The police came; I had to talk to a doctor. What I couldn't figure out when I was a kid was why I had to go to the doc. I mean, my father was the one with the problem; he needed to be in jail, but he never hit us again. He couldn't raise his arm; otherwise, he probably would have continued the abuse." Babe had replayed that night in his mind many times, but it was the first time he verbalized the ignorance of the justice system. They should have imprisoned Gino Vicarelli; instead, Babe had to go to counseling for a long time. *What of Gino's rage? Nadda.* There was satisfaction in his soul he had taken care of business.

The people who abused those victims in the metal warehouse were the ones needing the most horrific punishment. What they did to the victims was incomprehensible. There wasn't any form of torture sufficient enough. Babe could feel the heat rising from his chest up his neck to his face. He needed to release the confined anger, channeling it in the right direction. T-Train would feel his wrath. *He will be one dead motherfucker.*

"Jacob, if you want to talk to someone, let me know. Give me your word. You know, your word is a special bond, which means you will do everything to keep the oath or promise you made. I give you my word. I will do everything possible to get the people who abducted y'all, orchestrated the abuse, and profited off your body. What happened to whoever they brought to the ship is detestable and against G—" Here it was coming up again. 'God.' A quest he'd chase at another time.

Reflecting on his thoughts while away from Trinity and in the custody of the cartel, he clearly remembered speaking to the presumed real or imaginary God on several occasions. The thing was, all his pleas came true. *More research required.* His heart rendered a nod in acceptance. The plight was his internal struggle and not fodder for anyone else.

Jacob hadn't taken his eyes off Babe. "I'll think about the headshrinker; I give you my word." He took Babe's hand, and they shook on it. "That's even better than a pinky promise, which is such a girl or little kid thing to say." Babe chuckled and muttered pinky promise under his breath. He ushered Jacob off, followed by repeating Ruthie's instructions: bath, then bed.

After an extended visit with Ruthie, he headed toward Toledano Street. Ten-thirty should be late enough. Most respectable people were preparing for bed or dozing in a recliner in front of the television.

As kitted as his truck was, it would be hard for someone like T-Train to pass up the opportunity, no doubt. He slowly drove as he approached S. Prieur, pulled to the corner on an angle, threw a rag from the backseat over the license plate, and crouched by the driver-side rear tire as though inspecting it. Ten minutes passed, and there was no interested party; he moved to the right rear tire and repeated the inspection process. He didn't want to make a presence with his size, but then again, Clive wasn't a small man by any stretch. Driving down the block, four men stood around a man sitting on a stoop, passing a pipe. They glared at the truck as it passed. The plan might have worked if he had waited another fifteen minutes. He'd have to come back another night.

Babe turned on the radio as he headed to Louie's. Given the hour, he knew there'd be a crowd, and his visit would be short. His adrenalin pumped through his body. He couldn't wait to have her alone. His mind drifted to intimate times they'd had, then flashed like lightning to the shower, the snake, the abduction, and it roiled in his belly. Chop had even ruined his fantasies; he was enough to destroy a wet dream. *Fucking Chop.*

Meandering through the Quarter, he stopped as a truck the same size as his pulled out, leaving a good parking spot. They exchanged man waves with an extended forefinger and snap of the wrist.

DANCING WITH THE DEVIL

Babe leaned against the door jamb and watched as Trinity and Finn thrilled their guests. The money from what she had told him had been outstanding. Thoughts flashed through his mind of how happy Antoine might be seeing his baby girl putting on such a show. Odds were he'd be extremely unhappy. He wondered if he knew.

She spotted him and pointed to where he usually sat, and sure enough, she had a reserved sign in front of his barstool. He broke out in a full, crooked smile and could feel his eyes glistening with heat emanating from the south side of his belt. He'd stay for a short splash of Glenlivet.

His drink was before him in no time, and he pointed to her and at himself, raising his eyebrows. She indicated by flashing her fingers she'd be off at midnight, so he decided to stay and enjoy the sights.

Trinity wore his favorite jeans and the Louie's ragged-edged tee tied under her breasts. She was exposing more than usual, and he wasn't sure he liked other men ogling at her. Sweat glistened on her body, enhancing the ripples of muscle in her arms and abs. He wanted her in a most carnal way. Babe's thoughts consumed him. He imagined their bodies intermingling but watched Finn move with her in their choreographed act—their bodies too close for comfort. Knowing Finn, he knew there wasn't an ounce of disrespect or sexual innuendo. Or was there? Their routines had been polished to perfection, and the guests tipped well. He watched as Trinity and Finn's eyes locked. Was it silent communication regarding the performance, or was there something more? He shamed himself for such irrational thoughts.

Midnight finally came, and he watched as she grabbed her bag and slung it across her shoulder, then leashed Gunner, who was under the bar in a cubby hole. The ever-growing crowd had changed his once comfy spot encircling Babe's stool. For such a massive dog, he could coil into a small circle of fur. Babe walked outside and waited on the sidewalk for them. Gunner pulled the leash to get to the big man, creating a wake for her to follow. She weaved through the crowd, and he saw where a few people might have been too handsy; he felt a rumble of displeasure in his throat. On reflection, he should have escorted her out, ensuring there would be no untoward touching. He realized he was letting his mind ramble with out-of-control ideas—it wasn't good for anyone.

Babe ruffled Gunner's coat, getting into the pup's excitement. Trinity nearly jumped into his arms. "I have missed you, my handsome man. It is totally weird not having you at the bar. But before another second goes by—" She pulled him to her and kissed him with a long, hard kiss. Instantly, any thoughts other than her flew by the wayside. "I want to hear about everything. So much has happened. Every day is the same pretty much for me at Louie's."

"I'll fill you in on everything after a moment of your undivided attention." She was bouncy like a school kid and tried to jump up on him. "You want me to carry you?" He stooped, and she climbed on his back. She was hardly any weight, and he found the picture in his mind to be funny. It provided as much laughter as when she asked him to flex. His heart pounded with elation. She brought something to the table he'd never had, making his insides feel like Jell-O. He guessed it's what people meant by putty in someone's hands. He was most definitely putty.

They made it to her place, then both peeled off their clothes and embraced a shower. Their hands caressed each other, and what started as giddy fun turned into a most sensual interlude, moving from the bathroom to the bed. Somewhere between ecstasy and exhaustion, they fell asleep.

The morning came. Babe quietly slipped from the bed dressed, and he and Gunner headed to his apartment for his morning workout and then off to work. His exercise routine had changed due to his injury, which was taking a long time to heal. Perhaps the wound would have recovered if he had stopped getting in brawls or jumping from roofs and moving cars. With the advent of the Conti project, he found he needed the truck and not just travel on foot. Yes, a motorcycle would be handy, but where would Gunn sit?

His phone vibrated, propelling him from thoughts to real-time. "Vicarelli."

"Jarvis, here. You have a chance to talk to your boy?"

"Yes, sir. Thirty people ranged from five to adults. And they are servicing a cruise ship. Who do—"

"Can we catch lunch?"

"Sure."

"Port of Call, one?"

"See you then." Disconnect. While Babe admired the sense of urgency, he hadn't had a chance to discuss it with Trinity or get an okay from Glenn. Perhaps it would be the icing on the cake, and he'd be out of a job. He couldn't blame him. This kind of here one day gone the next would have never flown with him. Trinity would have understood the urgency once he had explained the situation to her in detail or as much as he could. He'd have to formulate a list of questions like what would they do once they got the kids, and wouldn't a raid warn others they were onto the game? Babe felt inadequate. Nothing in his training had prepared him for this, and then he corrected himself; yes, he had been. There had been several rescue operations in Africa and Afghanistan; they moved small villages. The difference was it hadn't been personal like this. He pulled by the dumpster and got out with Gunner on his heels.

Babe didn't hesitate and got straight to work. Glenn tried to engage in small conversation, but Babe was more silent than usual. "Vic, you okay?" Glenn asked.

"Yes, sir, got a lot of things on my mind." He briefly responded.

"Getting cold feet about your promise ring?" he laughed. "Buddy, you can talk to me anytime. I know the Noelles inside and out." *Buddy? Hm.*

"Nothing like that. One day, we'll sit and talk over a beer." *And pigs will fly.* Once again, he didn't want his stuff across broadband and the way it felt; too many people knew already. Very few people could understand what he saw, and he hadn't gone into the warehouse. He knew it was hot as hell there, even inside air-conditioned places. It was plain old hot, and he couldn't fathom the heat from all those bodies huddled inside the tin house of cards. One bottle of water per person wasn't enough to hydrate any of them. He felt certain people died inside the warehouse from the heat, dehydration, malnourishment, or abused bodies.

Around noon, most of the men clocked out for lunch. Glenn stayed behind. "You not eating today?" he seemed curious. "Look, from now on, you don't need to come here; focus on Conti. You're not gonna miss any excitement, have no fear. Some of the other men will be closing here and heading toward you." The food truck pulled up, "What you gettin'?"

"Meeting a friend at Port of Call at one," Babe said with little to no emotion, like it was a perfectly normal thing for him to do. Glenn merely nodded and ordered his hamburger and fries.

At one o'clock, he walked into the establishment. Jarvis was sitting at a table in the corner with a baseball cap and glasses. Babe didn't recognize him until he gestured. "Incognito?"

"Yeah, I change it up. Unfortunately, it's one of the problems; a pedo or runner could be your next-door neighbor or a normal guy at work. There isn't a club uniform or a neon sign above their head. There's a department strictly and constantly looking for child porn. Sometimes, we have to play the role; I know it sounds disgusting, but you gotta get in tight to get the information. Building trust is important. These people are suspicious of everyone not in the club or new faces they don't know to be in the club." They ordered. "So how many? You said thirty?"

"Yes, thirty. Jacob said it depends on if the cruise ship is in. If so, the ones they pick get to shower, comb their hair, and dress in better clothes instead of the rags they usually wear. Then, he said, a boat picks up the ones going to the party ship and delivers them. He knew so much of the detail; I know they'd picked him at least once, but I didn't ask him."

The conversation went on for another twenty minutes until their food arrived. Jarvis asked between bites, "So, all you want to do is get those people out of the warehouse, and that's it, no other rescues?" The way he asked wasn't judgmental, just honest.

Babe had to think it over and took another bite of his hamburger. "I have a feeling some other street kids from New Orleans are in the tin box. I feel like I am starting to have a life and—"

Jarvis held up his hands. "No worries. This isn't everyone's bag, and it can be dangerous. You're putting your life on the line."

Babe interrupted, "I have no trouble with the life on the line part of the equation. I've been on the front line in terrorist compounds cartel businesses; I'm not afraid of putting my life on the line. I've never experienced normal, even as a child. I went from high school to college, law school, and then the Marines. I guess I'm odd. I want something I can hold onto for once in my life. I was an abused kid, not sexually but physically, mentally, and emotionally, until I was twelve. I crippled my father by beating him with a chair. He abused my mother and me. I put an end to the physical."

Jarvis said, "Wow," nodded, and continued to eat, but Babe could see the gears grinding. "There is this one guy who is fucking amazing. The measures he's taken to rescue one kid are unbelievable. It's his calling, and I guess that's part of it. God calls all of us for different purposes, and that's his and now mine." He took a sip of his drink. "I'll help you with the warehouse. I know the ins and outs and will handle all that; I need you for the directions to the place and the numbers, depending on how many guard them. I have a small team, and we'll get it done or try. Once we've got 'em, I'll take over from there and run them through our system. Sound okay?" Babe nodded and asked for the check.

"This is on me, and I can donate money to your cause if that'll help," Babe added.

"Hell, yeah, that'll help. We will take anything. I'm gonna give you some pictures and see if your boy saw any of them. Text me either yes or no, nothing else." Babe paid the bill, took the pages of pictures, and left. He figured Jarvis would leave after he was gone. It all seemed so clandestine—*the nature of the beast,* he thought.

When he arrived at Conti, he recognized three men from the other job site working with the Hispanic workers he'd already met. In one and a half days, they had made impressive progress. The dumpster was gradually getting filled hour by hour. He hoped Glenn would be pleased with the progress.

On his way home, he stopped by Louie's. Trinity would just be coming on, and they'd have a moment to talk. She looked surprised to see him. He was dusty with smudges on his face. Somehow, she found his work-look sexy. "Do you wear a hard hat?"

He squinted in puzzlement, "Yes," he answered slowly, like waiting for the other shoe to drop. "Why?"

"I bet it's so gritty and sexy." She smiled and batted her eyes with her hand on her hip.

He sat. "Oh, to be sure, it's gritty. A two-finger pour—"

Her head waggled from side to side, "As if I don't know what you drink, Babe Vicarelli." She handed him the tumbler of Glenlivet. "So, my man, why didn't you go home? I'm guessing you're not going to be around here too much tonight." She continued cutting lemons, oranges, and limes. "You eating here tonight or with the boys?"

"Not sure. Do you have a second? I have some pictures I'd like to show you, and tell me if you recognize any of these people." He pulled the curled papers from his rear pocket. Trinity thumbed through and stopped at one picture of a young woman.

"Not poz, but I think she's a, um, lady of the night." Babe grabbed the pen off her tee shirt, catching a glimpse as the shirt pulled away from her skin. He registered a big smile and marked the picture of the woman. Then she came to a boy about ten or twelve and said he was one of the group Shep would feed. Babe put a check next to his picture. She didn't seem to recognize any others. The next stop was Chestnut. He ordered skins and spent an hour telling her about his thoughts on the warehouse kids. She seemed keen on his plan. "So, just that one time, right?"

"Yes, ma'am. I told the guy I wanted a real life for a change. He said it was a calling from," and he looked at the food, "God." She nodded. He downed the rest of his drink, "I gotta get to Chestnut. Any problem sleeping there Sunday night? Like we'll head over there after church," he sighed. "They go to church with Ruthie."

Trinity leaned forward with a pucker. He lightly kissed her and left.

The ride to Chestnut was getting routine. Ruthie and the boys were happy to see him, but it was no longer a revelry of surprise. "You need to get in the shower as much as the boys. You're filthy. Stand outside and pat yourself. I'm taking you have more work tonight?" She walked into the kitchen; Babe followed. "Chicken and dumplins tonight."

"Jacob upstairs?" She pointed to the dining room. He entered and asked Jacob to sit in the living room with him. He could hear Ruthie's gruntled feelings about his filthiness and being in the living room. *Too bad.* "Look through these pictures. Do you recognize any of these people from the warehouse? Put a check on the page if you do." He checked the ones Trinity had and five more—four kids and one woman. "Thank you. Now, let's get out of the living room before we get dragged by the ear." Babe winked at him. Walking to the dining room, he texted Jarvis. "Yes." His phone rang.

Jarvis spoke, "We leave out Monday; be home no later than Wednesday. Book your flight."

"I'll book 'em both."

"No need brotha; we got a team of six, seven counting me." The flight was leaving at seven on Monday morning. From what he said, most cruises started Wednesday and ran through Friday or Sunday. Not only were these people drugging it up, but they were passing the kids along to each other, meaning each child or woman got banged multiple times. The turnover was what made it such a lucrative business. Babe felt like he was going to vomit.

Undoubtedly, he zoned during dinner, thinking about Jacob and the nightmare he lived through. The boys were chatty, so his quietness went without notice or comment. It was too early to go T-Train hunting. He wondered what the boys watched on TV. Once they had their baths, they returned to their rooms; Chris went into another room to talk to his girlfriend. He knocked on the door frame, pulled up a wingback, and watched some mindless show Reg and Jacob were watching. He felt himself nodding off and headed downstairs. "We have any sodas around here?" She shook her head, saying it was bad for the boys. *Point taken.* He sprawled the best he could on the sofa, set the alarm on his phone, and dozed.

It seemed only minutes when the alarm went off. The house was silent and battened down for the night. He quietly left for Toledano Street. He pulled up where he had the night before and began the routine of checking the tires again. Toward the end of the ten-minute inspection of the passenger rear tire, footsteps approached behind him. The intensity triggered his senses into high alert; by the sound, he couldn't determine how many people might be coming for the attack. As he could almost feel the kinetic energy, he sprung up and turned. The man and two sidekicks stood copping major attitude and posturing. The leader smiled; the glow from a dim street lamp caused a glimmer on his full grill. He had T-Train.

"Your ride is dope," he said with a hand in his right pocket. "Boy, you picked the wrong skreet to ex-a-mine the treads. Keys," he demanded with a snap of his fingers as the two other men stepped forward.

"Don't pick a fight you can't win." He wanted someone to swing or pull out a weapon. His entire body tingled. Payback was gonna feel good.

"Oh yeah." Grill mouth pulled out a knife. The three descended upon him, and as he had in a previous incident not far from Louie's, Babe maneuvered the guy so he was facing the other two, turned the knife and plunged it into one of the sidekicks, and nailed the other in his solar plexus with a quick kick, hurling him three feet onto his back. The man with the knife in his gut stepped backward, sputtering coughs and nearing shock. Babe didn't feel the need to warn him about a bleed out. He hoped he would. Since he hadn't touched the weapon, the recent prints on the handle were from the grill mouth.

Before neighbors got curious, he flexed tightly in a suffocating choke hold. A snap of the neck would have been faster, but with the recent conversation with Trey and Max, it wasn't a viable option. Mission accomplished, the pieces of excrement were now a non-issue. The sprawled-out man had a pool of blood underneath him from hitting his head on the rough-edged concrete and a blank stare of death in his empty eyes. There were no prints, no DNA, no trace to his knowledge. If someone saw, they hadn't screamed, turned on the outside lights, or approached. He lingered not a second more and took off in his truck. All in all, the incident took eighteen minutes of waiting, then five minutes tops in defense. He pulled around the block and headed to Louie's, still in his dusty togs.

HEART TO HEART

Surprisingly, the crowd thinned early for a Friday night, and things had slowed substantially by the time he got to Louie's. Shep was long gone, the kitchen had been closed for a couple of hours, and the extra staff dismissed; it was a perfect opportunity to talk to Trinity about the conversation with Jarvis. She walked around the bar and sat on the stool next to him. "Big guy, you look like someone about to burst with information. What's the scoop?"

Finn waited on the few customers coming up for a cocktail. Babe watched him closely. "I think young Finn has the hots for you. I don't mind; it's okay, I understand. I have the hots for you, too." He coughed out a laugh. "Oh, my girl, you're not going to like this; I'm not so sure I like it, but I appreciate the urgency of this guy, Jarvis. We fly out for Colombia Monday morning at seven to rescue all thirty people from the metal building. He has the contact to transport them out of there once we have them. My job is to show him the way and fend off anyone who tries to stop us. It won't be only me; he has a team. Jarvis said the latest we'll be home is Wednesday. Do you think I should tell Glenn the whole story? If it were me and one of my employees, I would've fired my ass months ago." He circled the rim of his glass with his finger, looking at the amber liquid inside. She could tell he was having one of his internal debates and stayed silent for a minute or two, then cleared her throat.

"Finn, can you pour a little red for me?" He turned, winked at her with a smile, poured the wine, and brought it to her. She took a long sip.

"Babe, he knows it was the cartel who abducted you. I was going insane without you and went to the construction site because I knew it would smell like you. I needed something that was of you. Whenever I mentioned to anyone I was worried you were dead, they dismissed me. Glenn listened and took me seriously. He didn't poo-poo me like everyone else. He agreed it could be a distinct possibility if not a probability. Yeah, I'd say you're safe to tell him what you want—all or bits and pieces, it's up to you." Babe ordered another two-finger pour. "You're pensive about this. What is your hesitation? You getting bad vibes?"

He shook his head and wanted to explain about the cruise ships and passing the kids from one sicko to another, but she'd probably be sick. It's like he needed to purge the image from his mind; it seemed to reach his soul. The child he kept picturing was Jacob. If he hadn't stopped Chop, that would have been the destiny of Chris and Reg, as well. His stomach churned with cramping pain. His ill feeling reminded him of Trinity. "Are you feeling better? I'm sorry, I forgot with all this other shit going on."

She took another sip of her wine. "I'm fine. It passed. I told you Emetrol is like a miracle potion." He had enough fish in the fryer; he didn't need anything else. The rest of their conversation was light, joking with Finn and tossing a toy for Gunner. The Elvis song, Can't Help Falling in Love, started playing. "I know you don't dance, so you say, but this is slow; please dance with me." She cocked her head to the side. He stood, took her in his arms, and danced to the song. While her head barely reached his sternum, she put her ear to his chest, listening to the beat of his heart. He stroked her hair and held her tight. Babe looked at her and sang the last line. Her eyes widened and became glossy with tears. "I didn't know you could sing. By the way, sport, you dance just fine."

"Whatever, but I certainly don't gyrate like you or Finn." He found the whole thing amusing, his gut bubbling with something good; he couldn't define it or put his finger on it, but it was good.

A fast, hip-hoppin' song came up next; Babe turned to sit. "No, at least try; I promise I won't laugh. You're a white boy; you're not supposed to be able to dance." She laughed as she grabbed both his hands. "Just do what I do." She pulled his head to her and whispered, "You know how to dance in the sheets, so, boy, you got rhythm."

"No, Trinity, it's out of my zone." She pouted but started dancing around him, rolling on his body. He grabbed her hips, pulled them close, and moved with her body for a minute. "Good enough?" She smiled with her mouth open, then danced by herself. "Girl, all you're missing is the pole."

Babe sat and watched her as she drifted, letting the music take her to her happy place. At the end of the song, she plopped next to him. "Babe, you can dance; you're not letting yourself. Maybe, if I got you tipsy, like one too many two-finger pours," she winked at him. "Then, after dancing, I could take advantage of you when we got home." She feigned a gasp with her hand over her mouth, then giggled.

He had to laugh at her silliness. He pulled her closer. "I don't get tipsy, buzzed, drunk, or one too many ever. Never. I have to keep my self-control intact, or who knows what damage I might do? We can dance when we're alone; how 'bout that?" He mimicked her feigned gasp, putting his big mitt over his mouth. Trinity belly-laughed herself to tears. Time was winding up for them to close.

Upon getting home, Trinity wiggled out of her clothes. The energy her job required always left her sticky with perspiration or, as her mother would say, aglow because women didn't sweat. Babe had become accustomed to the peeling slick clothes from her body, traipsing to the washing machine naked and then into the shower. He removed his clothes and put them in with hers before saying, "I had an idea; it's okay if you don't like it; it's just a thought." She shouted from under the spray of the shower to get on with the point. *Hm.* "When my lease is up, which is soon, I won't renew and move in here with you. I'll pay the rent; it's not like I'm a leech. The only thing is, I'd have to install a chin-lift bar and find somewhere to set up my weights." Silence.

He stood under the spray with her. "I don't pay rent, but if you moved in, my dad might change the agreement. He doesn't like the living together thing, but since I have a ring, maybe." He smiled and leaned in for a long, tender kiss. Babe picked her up, and she naturally wrapped her legs around him. "I see that look in your eyes, Babe Vicarelli. What's going on in here?" She tapped the side of his head. He slid her body onto his. The passion mounted, both with muffled sighs and moans. The crescendo was punctuated by an "Oh, God, yes" from Trinity and a primal groan of satisfaction from Babe. "Ah, now I know what was going on in there," she commented with a throaty rasp.

Trinity piped in as they started toweling off with several questions about him moving in. "If you don't want me to, I'm fine like it is. I figure we jump back and forth, and in the mornings, if we're not at my place, I have to leave earlier to get my workout time. You could always move in with me, either at the apartment or Chestnut."

"It's not that; there's also the option of Lakeview." Babe shook his head no.

"Negatory, lady. Too much bad, uh, juju." He raised his eyebrows, waiting for her reaction. Let's make the most of the next two days; I ship out Monday morning."

She cocked her head in contemplation, "Sure, why not move in here, at least for the time being. I know it seems like a big space, but it may feel smaller once there are two of us all the time. Let's take one moment at a time. While you're gone, I'm going to clean my room and make space in my closet and the bathroom for your things. I know you claim not to have much. You left two complete wardrobes behind with your endeavor with the Colombian people. What a waste." She turned the covers and climbed into bed. "Give us a kiss, big man, and then sleep, pronto. This li'l chick is exhausted."

Babe woke up late, around eight. He felt behind schedule. He dressed, grabbed Gunner's leash, and the two began the morning run. Like most Octobers, there were a few days where one might detect a breeze of Fall; no matter how fleeting, it felt good. He figured he'd forego the weight training as it would be a bit of a workout hauling it all to Trinity's. Maybe he should ask Antoine if he had any objections to him moving into her apartment and offer to pay rent.

Babe and Gunner took an elongated run as he postulated on Monday's mission. He needed to ask Jacob a few more questions—like how many people guarded them and whether they had automatic weapons slung over their shoulders. Had the boy seen cameras? Then, his mind moved on to things beyond what Jacob could know. Were people at Javier's monitoring activity at the warehouse? The security control room and Javier's private quarters were the areas he didn't see while at Casa Garcia. Given all the cameras and intense security when they arrived, he most likely had a state-of-the-art surveillance system and skilled team. The thought ran through his mind; he'd forgotten about meeting with Hurley and his friend, Pierce, for the celebrity babysitting. There was no honor in such frivolity. If it were political puppets, certainly they would have their own detail, same with foreign dignitaries. *No*, he reflected. *It sounds more like celebs taking themselves way too seriously. Okay*, he acquiesced; *some big names definitely need security.*

When they returned to her digs, Trinity had dressed and was ready to leave. "Where are you off to?" he asked. She held a long list of scribbles. She mentioned they needed to go to the grocery and to stop in at the house in Lakeview. While she watched the end of an NCIS episode, she sipped her coffee, waiting for him to shower and dress, which only took a few minutes.

All ready to go, he commented, "I've seen the series before. I like the characters; they're unusual. Things don't go as portrayed in real life, but it's the best resemblance I've seen as far as television depicting Marine code, at least the one guy with gray hair; nonetheless, it's TV, not real."

"Babe, you ever wear shorts?" He cocked his head to the side with curiosity and confusion; his eyes squinted with brows drawn together.

He opened the door and patted Gunner on the head with instructions to keep the bad guys out; they'd be home soon. "Every day, when I work out and run. What a weird question."

Trinity slapped his arm. "No, goofball, like to go to the store or out to lunch." She rolled her eyes. "Not just for exercise."

"No, why?" The question seemed to perplex him. "That makes no sense. Do you not like my jeans? There are clothes for hanging in the house or working out and proper clothes to wear when I go out." His thought was perfectly reasonable to him.

"So, you think I shouldn't wear shorts?" She nudged him in his belly.

"You're a woman, of course; you can wear shorts, dresses, and skirts."

She slapped him harder on his arm, "I never figured you for some sexist, misogynistic pig. I'm shocked." He was surprised; he had no idea what she was going on about. "What about the women you served with? Would you think they wear clothes other than fatigues and jeans?"

They walked through the hotel to the parking garage, where her car awaited them. "I never thought of them other than Marines. I guess I have seen one or two in something else; I don't know. I can't recall it. I've never really thought about it. Trinity, you wear whatever the fuck you wanna wear; it's all fine with me. I think maybe we should take my truck; I don't know how many groceries we'll fit in your sexy sports car. As it is, I'm gonna take up a bit of space." She insisted so he felt like he folded into the tiniest form he could, putting the passenger seat as far and low as it could go. "Hm, it's not as uncomfortable as I thought it would be, but I still don't know where we're gonna put groceries."

Going to the store with Trinity was an experience. It was almost like a date, and somehow she managed to fit everything into the matchbox, almost non-existent trunk and room behind her seat. Her eyes twinkled as she spoke. "You had fun? It looked like it. Now, I know what you like to keep in the fridge and pantry. Ya know, I can cook. You don't always need Ruthie or Shep to create tantalizing meals." She batted her eyelashes.

He grabbed her around the waist, engulfing her in his arms, "You are a tantalizing meal, ma'am." She planned a quick stop by her Lakeview house, and to his surprise, there was a realtor's sale sign in the front yard. When they entered, a cleaning service had taken care of any mess. The house had the same beach smell as her place in the Quarter. She had all new bedding in her bedroom. He hadn't ever looked around the house; he toured it with her—four bedrooms, five bathrooms, a living room, and an open kitchen looking into a quaint den. It was impressive. She had an office with a big desk.

"Now, why do you have an office?" Then he stopped realizing his words came out condescending. "I know." He slid her shorts and panties down and sat her nakedness on the desk, sliding her body to his face and staring into her eyes. Babe adjusted himself to enter her welcoming body. Between thrusts, he said, "This is why you have the office, just another playroom," and chuckled, trying to make light of his first comment. He'd never gotten in trouble for too much talking, but it seemed as though Trinity's propensity for chatter was rubbing off; only his filter malfunctioned, and things came out sideways.

"Marine, see the advantage; it's precisely why I have a desk, aren't you glad?" She grinned with a devilish glint. "Actually, for resale. While you were vacationing in Cartagena, I decided to put the house up for sale. The sign went in the yard this week." He watched her speak as though mesmerized by her. Looking at her sent chills through his body, resulting in an involuntary shiver. "Babe, I'm super tired. Can we get home so I can take a nap? I'm exhausted. You wore me out, boy." Trinity was never tired, or at least he'd never heard her say so until recently. Maybe she was still sick with Covid or the flu.

"Can I drive this mean machine?" He asked. They had to adjust the groceries, but he moved the seat back as far and low as it would go. She dozed on and off on the way to the Quarter and crawled into bed as soon as they got there, knocking out in minutes.

Babe started the arduous task of moving his weights, clothes, pictures, posters, computer, chair, and table. He left everything else, emptied the fridge, and called Denise, letting her know he wouldn't be renewing his lease and had left the furniture. She could lease it furnished if she wanted. If not, he'd donate it and be by to pick it up in a few days. She was thrilled to have it furnished, considering she had picked out all the pieces during his first week after signing the lease.

Four o'clock rolled around, and Trinity hadn't woken up yet, still nestled in the covers. Babe gently sat on the bed, stroking her face with light wisping touches. Gradually, she woke, stretching the sleep from her body. "Trinity, are you sick? I've never known you to tire like this. Maybe you have the flu or Covid. Call Shep—"

"It's Saturday; no can do, big guy. I'm fine, but thanks for letting me sleep." Slowly, she dressed and fixed herself for work. When she walked into the living room, she was taken aback by his things neatly stacked in the corner. "Wow, you've been a busy bee while I slept. Put your things wherever you need them. Also, feel free to hang your frames and posters. That reminds me, we need to get a professional picture of us. I don't have one photo of us together and none of you. Walk me to work?"

Trinity seemed happier than usual, which was something since she always had a carefree, easy-going way about her. "I'll stay for a few. I'll have my Glenlivet and a hamburger with skins, then head to set up my weights and install my chin lift. Where do you want it?" She answered wherever, but she'd prefer the door into the bathroom. He left after an hour of shooting the shit with Finn and watching Trinity gear up for the Saturday night crowd.

It took a few hours to set up his workout area in Trinity's dining area. The table looked unused, so he figured it wouldn't matter if he removed the leaves and made it smaller, thus fitting everything perfectly. It was time to head to Chestnut. The boys were cutting up in the backyard with some of the kids from the area. Ruthie came out on the back porch, not seeing him, and called out to the group, "Hands need to get washed. Line up, get you a plate, silverware, and a napkin. The buns, hot dogs, beans, and corn are on the island, then sit at the dining table. No starting food until grace, you hear me?"

Babe had to grin; she had a group of seven boys marching in step with no backtalk. He stood at the end of the line, all the boys looking over their shoulders at him. Although Babe had eaten, spending time with Chris, Reg, and Jacob would be good; plus, he'd see who they were hanging with. After eating, he'd spend a few more minutes talking to the younger about who guarded them in the warehouse and how many.

Chris looked at him, "Heya, big guy. Are you gonna eat with us? And don't forget you said you and your squeeze would be here tomorrow." *My squeeze? Trinity's gonna love that one,* he mused.

The line moved in an orderly fashion, and talk at the table was fun. A few of the boys teased Chris about his girl. He glanced at Babe, wondering if he remembered the condoms. As quick as their eyes met, the thought ricocheted through the big man's head. He knew two were in the console. He ran outside to the truck, pocketed them, and called Chris after they washed their plates. The guests left after dinner and a brownie, giving Babe a moment to hand off the packets.

"Jacob, I need a few minutes." They sat on the porch outside. "I know you don't like talking about this, but I need some information." The boy nodded and asked him what he wanted to know. "Were there people inside the warehouse guarding y'all with big guns?"

"No, sir. There were two guys outside with guns, but they mostly sat in chairs and got stoned. No one ever came by the place unless it was time to bathe for the cruise." The boy became quiet and thoughtful. "Do you know what they made us do?"

Babe bit the inside of his cheek. He wanted to hurt someone, really fuck them up. "I have a pretty good idea, and I'm sorry it happened."

He looked at the Babe and admitted with tearful eyes, "I have nightmares. I wake up screaming and crying. Chris and Reg know what happened; I didn't tell them, but they know, and it's the only time they don't rag me about crying. I think they told Miss Ruth because she always gives me extra attention and doesn't let the bigger kids pick on me. Can I go watch TV now?" They both stood, went inside, and Jacob said with painful sincerity, "I hope you get them all and maybe one day bust the ship. It would serve them right to go to prison." The little guy had a point.

While the focus was rescuing the kids, he knew there'd always be more kids to follow. The problem was the go-betweens and end-users. He flinched, balling his fists with a jutted jaw. Someone had to pay. Maybe he could unleash his inner demons by beating the piss out of all of them. While he'd like to shoot them, prison would be better; for sure, they'd get theirs. Pedophiles didn't do well in prison. Like him, inmates had a code.

Babe hoped they had not moved the victims to another location. He needed to let Jarvis know it was a distinct possibility since Javier knew he'd seen the place when he rescued the one. There was no doubt the driver told him. Since it had been a time since it all happened and he hadn't retaliated sooner, maybe Javier would think he settled when he returned home.

Babe put his feet up on the ottoman. "So, Ruthie, all going well for you? How's Clive doing?" She raised her eyebrows and pursed her lips.

"I heard you went to see my boy." Babe nodded. "The strangest thing happened. Those three boys tried to jack someone else's vehicle close by where they lived. Yes, those boys have always been trouble. Whoever the owner of the car was took all three of them out, can you imagine?" She shook her head. "I said to myself, my Clive has someone looking out over him that he didn't die, and whoever is watching him punished the boys who did him wrong. Don't it beat all? Something, huh?" She had a devilish twinkle in her eyes. While she had no proof, she had suspicions that her giant friend might know a little something about it.

"No kidding. What a mess. As they say, mess with the bull; sometimes you get the horns." He stood. "Have a good night, Miss Ruthie; I'm off to see my lady. We'll be here tomorrow night. I'll be out early Monday morning, and she'll probably stay in bed. I think she likes it here."

Trinity and Finn flipped bottles to each other. A large crowd of loud, obnoxious people entered Louie's. They stopped momentarily to take drink orders; Finn called them to Trinity. The rockin' music created a party atmosphere. A stout blond-haired man winked at her, then boldly said, "Hey, girlie, gimme some brown sugar." Finn's face showed anger, and he knew she would strike like a Cobra. Although she was tiny, she didn't put up with rudeness. She abruptly turned.

"Boy, you better watch your mouth, or you can take your merry self down the street. That's not the game in Louie's." The man reached over the bar, trying to grab her. One of the old-timers told the man he needed to apologize and take his nasty ass somewhere else.

"Fuck you, old man and girlie; you can't speak to me like that. It's been a long time since I was a boy, and some nigga chick like you, ain't gonna call me boy. Finn hit the button under the counter that flashed in the kitchen. Shep called nine-one-one and headed into the bar.

At first glance, the problem person stood out like a goat among the sheep. He walked up to the man. "Sir, this is my establishment, and I'm asking you to leave the premises."

"Oh, are you? Well, what if I don't wanna leave? Your little nigga bitch behind the bar insulted me." He passed no return; Shep grabbed him by the scruff of the neck, and two uniforms walked in as he was forcefully escorting him out. "Officers, this man has assaulted me. I want to press charges." Max was right behind the officers.

"The fuck you say. People don't get run outta Louie's very often, so mister, I'd take your sorry ass somewhere down the street before it gets ugly." The man was fighting to get away from the two uniforms. Max couldn't help but think he *would have loved to see Babe deal with this guy*. Trey came from the other direction.

"Sir, please step away from the door." Speaking to the uniforms, "Y'all let him go." He looked at the man. "What seems to be the problem, sir?" A couple of the man's friends came outside apologizing for their friend, who obviously had too much to drink. One man, a good-sized specimen, offered to bring his friend to the hotel and said there wouldn't be any more trouble.

"Charlie, you leave me alone. I ain't apologizing or going back to the Royal Sonesta. Sonny," he said to Trey, "you know who I am? My family is big in this town, and I'll have your job. What's your name and his," pointing at Max. "That sombitch cursed me; I want his badge number. You messed with the wrong man." Another one of his friends tried to take him by the arm, and the guy swung at him, landing the punch on Trey's shoulder.

"Sir, you have now committed battery." Between Max and Trey, they held him still long enough for one of the uniforms to cuff him and put him in the back of the unit. Once they drove off, Trey looked at Max, "What an asshole." The friends of the offensive man tried to reason with Trey and Max, explaining their friend wasn't usually so rude or inappropriate. Like always, a crowd of looky-lous gathered to watch the incident. "Break it up, everyone. Y'all head on out; nothing to see here." Trey sighed and rubbed his shoulder. "Dang it, that was one hell of a punch. Usually, drunks don't have such an impact. Bastard."

The drunk's group began dispersing; their friend had created such havoc it put a damper on the night. Finn approached Trey, "What is the guy's name? I've seen him in here before. He's never acted like such an asshole, but he always harasses Trinity. Not like tonight. Man, I almost went over the bar with the bat we keep behind for such purposes, but I knew y'all would handle it."

"I think he said he was related to the Beltons. I don't give a hearty crap who he's related to; you hit me, your ass is going to jail. His friend told him to go to their hotel, the Sonesta. I guess the group is staying there." His radio went off, "Gotta roll." He and Max took off.

Finn went behind the bar, and Trinity was still dancing and twirling bottles like batons. He asked if she was okay; she shrugged a shoulder and said absolutely. It was almost eleven; she figured Babe would be there any minute. Every few minutes, she'd look toward the door.

Finally, he rounded the doorway. Trinity felt a flutter in her heart and poured his two-finger Glenlivet. While it was still a party atmosphere, the decibel level had dropped to a reasonable volume. She left the bar momentarily, giving Finn a quick, sneaked second to fill Babe in on the excitement of the evening. He figured she wouldn't tell all.

"You got the information on this asshole?" Babe asked.

"Man, I wish you woulda been here. Trinity acted like she didn't care, but I knew it had to shake her. Ya know, she lets things roll off her, but I think this stuck, maybe not. I thought you might want the story if she doesn't tell you." Babe nodded with a wink. Having someone besmirch Trinity was something he didn't think he could tolerate well. He rolled with the flirting and misguided innuendos, but something negative was a different can of worms. Was it enough for him to do bodily harm, maybe before, but not now? He certainly could be menacing, but if provoked, that was an entirely different situation.

She returned with a little bounce in her step. "I am glad to see you. Sorry, but I had to hit the restroom fast; I didn't mean to run away as soon as you got here. It's been one helluva night. All good until some jackass starts up with racist talk. You get used to it, and I have no issues with the occasional slip of the tongue, but this guy was an asshole. Granted, he was drunk, but he showed his true colors. Who knows, maybe his wife ran off with a black man. I usually get Latino slurs, not black, but that's his problem. He's gotta stand before God just like I do. I guess I provoked some of it by calling him boy. I suppose it was like salt on a wound; I egged him on; he got pissed."

Babe sipped on his whiskey pour and watched her as she babbled about the jerk. He might have helped Max and Trey get him out of Louie's, but that would have been the extent of it. Name-calling was never the issue; it was the physical shit he wouldn't tolerate; somebody would pay. Babe looked for Gunner, and not unusual, he saw a curled ball of black fur with the tip of his pink tongue hanging out. Surprisingly, the dog didn't pick up on the negative vibe and react. It was good he didn't. His pup was a no-nonsense fighter when it came to Babe and Trinity.

The excitement at Louie's had calmed, and the late crowd was calling it a night. There were a couple of die-hards, but after calling them a cab and sending them on their way, the cleaning crew arrived along with the early shift. Trinity closed up the till, and they left right behind Finn.

DECEPTION, LIES, AND TRUTH

rinity seemed like a kid on Christmas when she walked in and saw his weights and how he'd set everything up. "Man, you're like a machine. You moved and set up in a few hours; wow." She hugged him with a thrilled squeal. "Oh, but yes, this is awesome. It is now our place, whatcha think? I like to watch you work out; it turns me on," she laughed with a gutsy big cat purr, rolling her tongue.

Babe took off his shirt, picked up one of the free weights, and curled it. "You mean like this?" She raced to the bedroom, and he followed close behind like two teenagers. Gunner sniffed all the new things in the apartment as they closed the bedroom door.

Once in the shower, he reminded her about Sunday with the boys at Chestnut. She then asked what about the conversation with Pierce. Could she sit in on the meeting? Fair enough, he agreed; she hadn't pushed meeting Jarvis. There were far more dangers in rescue than in babysitting.

The morning peaked in and woke his appetite, creating sounds of gut gurgles and growls. He needed food right then before church. He was already functioning on high alert with the upcoming flight the next day and the search and hopefully rescue in Cartagena. "Do you think Ruthie will mind if we take the boys to Mass and then my parents?"

"Not yet. Let's take one step at a time. Once I get through the mission and the victims are safe in the States, we can start thinking about domestic stuff. How do you think your father will handle having three street urchins at his house?" After tucking in his shirt, he zipped his jeans and threaded his belt. She threw on a tight skirt and form-fitting top. Babe couldn't help but notice she looked healthier rather than skinny, with every bony prominence protruding. What was it about him? Gunner gained weight hand over fist and was now a sizeable canine weighing ninety pounds. Trinity probably put on five pounds, which would be like him gaining twenty pounds. Her frame was so tiny. "Girl, you look good, not that you haven't always been beautiful, but your body has filled out some, and your skin seems brighter." He ran his hands over her as he leaned in for a kiss denied.

"Thanks, Vicarelli; you're saying I'm getting fat." He began stuttering and backpedaling, denying any such thing. "No, sir, you're not gonna crawfish out of this." She hugged his waist and looked into his eyes. "I have gained a couple; it makes those damn painted-on jeans tighter, but I know you like looking at my ass in those jeans."

"God, no, I mean, yes, I love looking at your ass. What I meant was you look even more beautiful. You make me want to grab you and pull you close." He scooped her butt and pressed their bodies tightly. "We better get going." Leaving Gunner with instructions, they left the apartment for church with plans of skipping the family meal. Gunner was a good excuse.

The morning passed, and nobody commented about him moving in with Trinity. The staff working Saturday afternoon knew for sure, as did her brothers. Bethany and her mom asked about the rings with their eyebrows raised. Antoine shifted his gaze at Babe, who acknowledged the stare with a nod and commented they'd speak later in the week if it were okay. Evidently, it was and the end of the issue.

Following church, they passed by the apartment, got Gunner, and headed to Chestnut. Ruthie was up to her elbows in preparing a full fare for Sunday dinner—standing rib roast, whipped potatoes with gravy, peas, a salad, and a chocolate cake for dessert. The boys seemed like regular kids from average homes, without signs of distress. Ruthie told Trinity and Babe that Jacob still had nightmares, but they had diminished some. "It's amazing the kid has come through as well as he has, " Trinity commented. "It took me some time to get over my assault." Ruthie put her hand on her hip, ready to hear the story and tell it she did. Ruthie put her hand to her mouth, slowly shaking her head, telling her how much courage it took to go through something of such a nature, and thanked God for Babe.

The phone vibrated on the counter; it was Pierce Kelly. "Where do you want to meet?" He asked.

"Say Fat Harry's in thirty minutes?" Babe answered, and they hung up. "I feel like I'm cheating on Shep going to another bar." She found the comment humorous. He had her up against the counter in the kitchen, kissing her.

Ruthie came in, turned around, and excused herself. Trinity broke out laughing. "Ma'am, please, don't leave."

A few minutes later, she returned to the kitchen. "I don't want to get all up in your business. I think it's sweet, and I know Mister Rune woulda thought so too. He was always telling me if his grandson could find a good woman, his tongue would loosen all the words he kept hidden in his heart. Oh, I heard about the sort of man your father was and all he put you through, poor baby. Your mother was a majestic lady and shoulda popped him right in his nasty mouth. You know your Farfar, is that right, dawlin'?" Babe nodded. "He wanted to kill that man. Mister Rune seen him maybe a year ago and said the man looked sick, so your grandad took pity and didn't run him over. He was skinny, hunched over, with a permanent scowl on his face. The old guy was funny to the core, especially when he imitated people. What a character! Not trying to speak ill of—"

Babe put his hand up to stop her. "No offense is taken. He was a no-good, mean bastard, no doubt about it. Ruthie, we have a meeting; it shouldn't last long and is down the avenue a short distance. We'll be back soon and then plan to watch TV with the boys." She shooed them out and said she'd see them when they returned.

Traffic was light on St. Charles, and they made it to Fat Harry's in less than ten minutes, parked, and started for the bar. "What's this guy like?" Trinity asked.

"Don't know. Pierce says it's some easy cakewalk, like babysitting celebrities and politicians. Anytime I hear something like that, I expect the worst. It was always the pain in the ass, no worries, kind of mission that went sideways. A fuckin' shitstorm. We're gonna meet the guy in charge. I don't know his name off the top of my head. Maybe Pierce told me; I don't remember. My mind is more on tomorrow. I have a feeling it's gonna get dicey. Jarvis was upfront about the dangers, but nobody would ever find the warehouse if they didn't know exactly where to look."

They turned into the open door. "This place never changes," Trinity laughed. "We used to hang out here, me and my friends. I used Bethany's driver's license to get in. I don't think we look alike, but I guess our skin and hair color are the same. If someone had looked close enough to see her eyes were blue, I'd been shit out of luck."

A man approached them. He was thirty-ish, had sandy hair, was attractive, about five-ten, and thought way too highly of himself. "Are you Vicarelli?" Babe nodded slightly with an intense glare. "Who do you have here?" He stood a little too close for Trinity's liking, and she didn't like the way he was scoping her.

"My wife. I thought she needed to be in on the conversation since she has to deal with the boys." *I need to put this guy down like a rabid dog; he's looking too close and eyeing her bits way more than necessary. She's beautiful, but dude, come on.*

Trinity put her hand out to shake his, "And who are you?" She asked in an almost demeaning manner.

"Come sit, y'all. Beer's on me. I have someone I want to introduce you to. His name is Nolan, and he never gives his last name; I'm not sure it's his real name." *For fuck sake, what is this? My answer is getting to be a fast no.* He was kissing the guy's ass. They approached a table with a balding, pudgy man with bulging fish eyes and a pad of lined paper in some plastic folder. "Nolan, this is the dude I told you about. He's perfect for the position. What'd I tell ya? My source was right on target." He was like one of those fucking dogs that bounced and yipped with a squealy noise. The man raised his eyebrows with a double pulse and a cheesedick smile. "Am I right, or am I right?"

Mr. I'm-not-using-my-real-name spoke in a low, deep whisper as though put on for theatrical purposes. "I suppose Pierce has told you about me." *Not really.*

Babe was direct. "I have questions, Pierce; how do you know Hurley?" The man started to fidget. *Not good.* "You served a couple of tours, I heard. Where? When?" The guy was almost trembling.

The boss spoke up. "We have a few questions for you. Do you understand how important this position is?"

Babe looked directly at both men from one to the other without a trace of a smile, maybe even a pissed look. "Let's clear the air, sir. I don't know what this douchebag told Hurley," pointing to Pierce, "But he's as much a Marine as I am a ballet dancer. Celebrities and politicians have hand-picked security, either Secret Service or PMC, private military contractors. This cloak and dagger is bullshit. Find yourself another yes-man."

"But, but, but—" Pierce's arms waved excitedly or panicky.

"Motherfucker, you don't know Hurley from days of serving, or the man I served with has lost his fuckin' mind. I'm out of here. Thanks, but no thanks." Babe stood, took Trinity's hand, and walked out. "What a waste of time." He pulled out his phone and called Hurley. "You on drugs? The motherfucker, Pierce Kelly, is a fuckin' scam artist. He no more served as a Marine than my dog has; maybe Gunner has more sense than both the morons I just spoke to. You served with that dumb-fuck, and now you work with him?"

"Wait, Vic, hang on. Yes, I served with Pierce Kelly; he's gone PMC because of a bad psych eval. He's like six-two, more salt than pepper, still built like a brick shithouse, but you can tell under stress, he might freak. I thought I'd help him out, and you might be interested, that's all."

"The guy I met with is not the man you described. Somebody is hacking into your organization or fucking something up, and his supposed handler is a muppet." He listened for a minute. "No, I don't have a picture of them," Trinity spoke up that she did. "Hang on; my lady took a couple; I'll send them to you. Listen, I'm not gonna do PMC except for a couple of people I've already worked with, but thanks for thinking of me. Sending the pics in a minute." They hung up. "You slick little chick, I didn't see you take any pics. Way to go, girl. Thanks." She sent the photos, which he forwarded to Hurley.

In minutes, his phone dinged with a message.
Hurley: What the fuck? No, he is not the man I told you about. I don't know who the hell they are. Sorry. Good luck with whatever you do.

Babe was thoughtful, his brows heavy over his eyes and his focus laser-like. The playfulness he had before vanished like caught in a windstorm. Trinity stayed silent, not knowing what to say, so silence was the perfect tool. She attempted to match his stride, but he was in the zone, and she trailed behind. She jogged to catch up, and it was then he realized he had gone into his head. "Sorry, Trinity, you don't need to run; I'll slow down." He attempted a one-sided smile, but it was greatly lacking. He touched the middle of her back; it helped ground him. The tightness in his chest was loosening; he felt his breaths calm from a raging bull to the quiet of a still night.

"I was beyond pissed with Hurley; I don't think I would have texted him otherwise and thought the motherfucker had lost his wits. Glad he answered. I don't get what those people were up to; why con me? Were they waiting to ask me to help fund the program or something? Fucking scammers. Someone from his group on the inside fielded the crazy. He needs to get out of there, but it's not my problem." He returned to his silent thoughts, but she could almost hear the gears grinding. He stopped, turned towards her, and took her by the elbows, "Tomorrow is the real deal, not some shameless bullshit."

After climbing in the truck, she kissed him gleefully and said, "So, you look at me as your wife?" Her smile spread across her face. "It sounded good coming out of your mouth."

He started the engine and pulled into traffic, which on St. Charles moved at a reasonable speed, honoring the gentility of the area. "The fucking asshole was drooling and probably shooting a wad as he looked at you. He's lucky I didn't pop him in his mug. Slimy bastard," he huffed.

His crudeness amused her. If anybody else spoke the way he did with the thoughts he had, she'd vanish like a puff of smoke. Somehow, his language and odd expressions fit him. He knew enough to curb his delightful observations and analogies around most people. She giggled to herself, trying to imagine him and some of his Marine warriors conversing. If censored, it would probably sound like bleep, bleep, bleep-bleep. "Babe, you have such colorful descriptions. Has anyone ever told you before? Do you realize the things you say?"

He turned, looked at her, then looked over his shoulder at the avenue, glancing at her. "I don't get what you mean?" His statement made her snortle. "Now that's attractive. I suppose you'll start farting at whim, my lady-like Miss Trinity." She shoved his arm.

"As if. No, I'm talking about your motherfucking, fucker, shooting a wad, and all in one conversation, but there have been many descriptive' expletives. I can't think of any others off the top. I've watched some war movies, and they always depict y'all with harsh language; not saying I like to watch those kinda movies very often. I always knew when Joey had been

149

hanging with his cop friends, everything was F-bomb this and F-bomb that. Maybe it's a guy thing."

Babe stayed quiet but then burst into a bellow of laughter. "Maybe so, but genteel Trinity, you use your fair share of profanity. Maybe you don't motherfuck with the best of 'em, but you certainly F-bomb. Finn cracks me up; he's always correcting himself; the *ff* comes out, but he quickly substitutes some other word." They pulled into the driveway inches from the garage door.

Trinity radiated happiness. "Finn is sweet. The first night we started the act, I kissed him. I didn't mean to; it just happened."

"You what?" He looked at her sideways. "Anything else I should know?"

She bit her lip, waiting for a burst of anger or a who cares attitude. Breezing past her admission, "I hadn't been at work for a couple of months. I was sick, depressed, and wanted to die when I thought you were dead. Finn picked up my hours, and once I had my shit together, I didn't want to pull the rug from under him. I know he likes me but also knows I'm yours."

Babe responded. "If this is confession time, you won't like what I'm about to say."

She walked quickly ahead of him, spoke over her shoulder, and said, "Then don't say it, please."

They could hear the microwave running and then the sound of popcorn popping. "Y'all were faster than I expected. The boys are 'round the block, but I'll call Chris." She spoke into the phone, "Call Boy Chris." She waited as the phone rang. Finally, he picked up. "Time for you boys to come home." Silence. "What you mean, they aren't with you? Where are you?" She frowned. "You leave that girl's house, now. Get the two and come home. We'll talk later." Silence. "Well, kiddo, you better find them."

Babe said he had an idea where they were, and he and Trinity would fetch them. On the way to the boy's house who stole the bike, he told Trinity the story, and the woman instigated the thought of a wedding band. "How do I look?" She asked, then stopped at a parked car and checked herself the best she could in the sideview mirror. Babe was puzzled.

"You look great as always. What's with the mirror primping?" His head cocked to the side. "Is it because she—"

"Yes!" She held his hand. "Okay, let's get the kids." The mom was sitting on the porch and could see Babe's head above the azalea bushes, but she didn't see Trinity until after she'd wooed a hello, which abruptly stopped when she saw Trinity. Under her breath to Babe, his tiny lady, whispered, "Yes, bitch, he's mine." He held back anything to say to her remark.

Before he came into view, they could hear Chris hauling ass on the bike. Grunting, "fuck, fuck, fuck. Those little shits better be—" With saucer-wide eyes and a look of sheer fear, he saw Babe and Trinity, "Uh, h-hey, y'all. I was gonna get Reg and Jake; y'all didn't need to walk all that way." The woman introduced herself to Trinity and said hello to Babe. The boys hustled; before long, they were walking to Chestnut. Chris nervously babbled the whole way to the house.

Reg poked Chris in the spine, "Dude, you got busted," he jeered.

TROUBLE ON THE WAY

7he ride to the airport conjured thoughts of Javier, the bloodbath at the resort, and desperately wanting to get home to Trinity. He wanted a regular guy's life, yet here he was on a rescue mission—he had to; it hurt deep in his heart. Questions pummeled his brain. Would he run into Javier or any of his people? Were the victims still going to be in the warehouse, or was this a colossal waste of time and money? Jarvis had seemed good for the cause and was behind him one hundred percent. Babe respected the man and the calling he said he had from God. He tried to believe; he wanted peace, but too much had happened in his life. The belief in God was far-reaching. Trinity said, just believe. It was easier for her, but didn't she harbor anger toward the God entity that allowed the rape and beating? Hell, Babe was angry about it and couldn't let it go. What about all those people in the warehouse and the millions of others? Would a loving, caring, all-powerful God allow such misery and perversity? Thoughts for another time; he needed to be at the top of his game.

Jarvis was waiting outside the terminal with a crew of six people: five men and a woman. Everyone was smiling, but it was a group of intense warriors. Determination creased the lines of Jarvis's face. Dressed in black and camouflage, Babe fit in with their attire. "Vicarelli, I've checked our weaponry and cleared it for travel. With what we have, I dare say we won't be overmatched." He listed the firepower they had. Quiet as usual, Babe was getting in his head- space. Once onboard, the silence penetrated his gut. His brain started rambling, and he found himself inwardly addressing God. *If You are real, God, please be with us as we rescue the victims. I do have a few questions for You, and I guess in time, You'll answer them, or someone will. Protect the people we assist and the warriors fighting the battle of perversion, especially today. If, in fact, You do smite evil, there are a lot of people in need of smiting. I guess thank you, and please hear my words.* Even though it was internal and no one could hear, he felt conspicuous in the endeavor. He had a ton of questions for Jarvis but figured it would all shake out in time.

The flight was unremarkable, except it hadn't been delayed, like so many flights. Before he knew it, they arrived. The eight of them filed off the airplane in silence. Jarvis signaled a man and woman waiting for them, and they moved as a unit to an awaiting military vehicle. Sitting in the cab were two official-looking people, law enforcement, he speculated—their local contact.

"Jarvis, can I talk to the driver?" He nodded and led him to the driver. The two spoke in Spanish. "Ask him if he knows where Javier Garcia's compound is. I can direct him from there. We will pass the compound and go another ten clicks to a gravel and dirt road on the right. Go two clicks in, and the warehouse made like a house of metal cards is well-hidden behind heavy, overgrown vines and foliage. It's hard to see." Jarvis rattled off the translation, and both nodded. The driver used a radio and repeated the message to some other party; Babe suspected the vehicle they used to transport the people from inside the building.

He climbed in with the rest of the group. Memories flooded his mind; how many times had he ridden in the same kind of vehicle, lined on either side with warriors awaiting either warzone or transfer? His mind zoomed to the past and one of his last transports. Nothing could prepare someone for the feeling of a vehicle almost hit by a missile. The makeshift road before and behind them turned to rubble in split seconds, and their truck tumbled like a can kicked down the road. The noise was deafening, and expectations of utter chaos and fear remained at bay. There was nowhere to take shelter. Vallas had the launcher and sent a missile screaming toward the enemy aircraft—missed. Another attack was imminent; they were fucked. Vallas loaded up in record time and sent another streaming for a strike; this time, success. A flurry of fire exploded as fragments spread across the sky, falling to the ground in black, smoky trails. Without a vehicle, they were shit out of luck and started hoofing it. He communicated the disaster, and supposedly, another truck would be coming. Fifteen minutes later, a helo hovered with ropes and cables dangling to climb or be wenched into the helicopter. It was another Chop rescue. Too bad, he reflected, what appeared as a once brave and brilliant pilot succumbed to a lifestyle of drugs and had, in all probability, been a piece of shit all along—a junkie for the adrenalin high.

The woman spoke to him, "Marine?" He nodded. She smiled and responded with a nod. After a few brief words, they found their assignments were on opposite sides of the world. She shrugged. End of the conversation; nothing more to say, but he could tell they followed the same code. The air was thick with anticipation and tingling of readiness.

Looking out the canopied truck, he saw the wall surrounding Casa Garcia. Would he be a welcomed guest ever again? It felt like mere minutes when they turned onto the gravel road, shortly stopping. Jarvis jumped out, followed by the rest of the group. They crept toward the metal building. Babe's description was balls-on-accurate. They silently moved along the side. He saw through a small gap huddled masses of people. Out of nowhere, a school bus pulled behind the truck. Babe heard two gunshots, and then a flood of people came running from the building like ants from a pile. There were well more than thirty, aged from toddlers to adults.

The journey had only begun. The mass of people flooded onto the bus, cramming every person inside the vehicle, which tore backward and turned in a different direction than Babe anticipated. His heart bounded in his throat. Were they being moved to another hellhole? Where was the bus taking them? He wished he would have jumped on the bus. When their truck pulled out, it followed the direction of the school bus. He suspected the pedal was to the metal going as fast as possible bouncing along the road. Their military transport suddenly swerved to the side at an angle; the crew hustled out in double time.

The victims ran down the side of a sea-worn plunge, crossing the sand and loading onto a boat. Babe could tell there was no way there would be enough room for them all. Four of their crew jumped onboard, and they hauled ass out of there. Jarvis directed the remaining victims behind the bus and the angled truck, instructing them to run deep into the thick vegetation. The last thing Babe saw was a plume of dust fast approaching their location. The transport and bus were empty, and where the drivers had gone was anyone's guess. Hidden amongst the foliage, deep away from the road, were twenty-plus people from the warehouse and the remaining four rescue personnel.

Babe had no doubt the vehicles creating a cyclone of dust worked for Javier. The SUVs randomly pulled in, skidding to a halt, with armed men screaming and firing their guns toward the fleeing boat. It was a wasted effort; the rescue team and victims had surpassed the distance their weapons could reach. One of the men, dressed differently than the others, casually walked to the bus, entered it, and exited, looking at one of the other people in their group. He studied the vegetation, perhaps looking for the drivers. Babe recognized Seb; he withdrew deeper, camouflaged by the jungle. Everyone remained silent as though holding their breath. The moment was tense, every synapse in his body exploding to the next.

Jarvis called for backup when he saw the people piling on the bus. With Javier's army hanging out in the area, there would be no chance of an escape. No doubt, once the cartel soldiers returned to the compound, Seb or Javier would assign a small unit to patrol the area on the happenstance some of their investment didn't make it to the boat. While the coast appeared clear, Babe and Jarvis knew better. The hush of silence continued. Hours passed, then off in the distance, they saw headlights appearing to be a bus or truck, maybe an SUV. Was it coming for them? If so, it was too soon.

The lights approaching came to an abrupt stop. Echoing through the atmosphere was a distinct pop from a gun. Whoever was driving the vehicle was toast. The lights slowly rolled to the side. Moments later, the pursuit was on again, and a bus was headed straight toward the empty bus and truck. Some of the victims seemed antsy. Jarvis could not make them understand it wasn't a bus for them and to remain quiet. Two teenage girls broke through, running into the road, madly waving their hands, jumping up and down. The bus stopped, the door cranked open with the sound of metal against metal, and then one of the girls turned, signaling toward the rest hiding among palmettos, palms, and banana trees to follow. Babe, Jarvis, and the other two personnel tried to stop them, but it was too late. Three SUVs raced toward the bus. Men jumped from the vehicles and headed into the density of wild foliage. Jarvis grabbed two kids and ran deeper into the overgrowth. Babe followed suit, as did the other two rescuers, but they heard screams from the victims, who had followed the wrong signals from the teenage girls. The two children he was holding started to cry; he cupped his hands over their mouths and quieted them. Babe could hear heavy footsteps moving through the jungle and loud voices calling in Spanish. Jarvis threw the two victims he had to one of the other team members, leaving all but one weapon behind; he put his hands on his head and started to walk toward the voices. Babe had no idea what the men had said, but it must have been hideous enough threats to make Jarvis reconsider his position. Babe couldn't let him go alone and turned his two children to the other warrior.

Following Jarvis, Babe put his hands on his head in surrender. The future looked grim. He stepped in front of Jarvis, and as one of the cartel thugs went for him, Babe slipped through his grasp, turned, and snapped the guy's neck. If they were going to take him down, he was determined to take a few of theirs. He crept behind another, got him in a choke hold, and tightened as hard as he could, snuffing out one more. To his recollection, it left four or six, not counting the one from the driver's seat of the bus, holding the teenage girl at gunpoint.

Jarvis took Babe's lead and followed suit, taking out one more. The cold muzzle of a gun pushed against the side of Babe's skull. He heard the distinctive click of engagement. Instinct kicked in, and he knocked the arm with the gun upward, causing the shooter to fire but missed him, and Babe nailed the man in the throat with the heel of his hand. The man pedaled back a few feet and tripped, landing on a broken tree trunk impaling his body. *Four down.* Whether there were two more or only the driver, the situation was now in his control. In the craziness of it all, he'd lost sight of Seb. *Not good.* He moved to the periphery of the growth and spied Seb running for one of the SUVs.

Babe took off after him, almost catching up; he tackled the younger man, grasping his legs and throwing him to the ground. A scream pierced the air; he saw the driver holding a gun to the teenage girl, obviously threatening. The driver turned to face Babe's direction; Jarvis came out of the brush and fired a shot, hitting the driver in the head. The girl screamed louder, blood and brain matter splattered in her hair and on the side of her face.

Seb growled at Babe, "So we meet again. Did you think you could steal from Javier and get away with it? He will hunt you down and skin you alive."

Babe shrugged, "Probably." Seb's phone rang; it was Javier.

Babe snatched the phone and, with a touch of sarcasm, said, "Hello, Javi."

"You are a man of your word, Captain. You told me you would come for them. Before you get yourself and all of them killed, let's talk. Come to Casa Garcia as my guest. I will let everyone go freely if you—"

"Deal. Are you a man of your word?" Babe asked.

"You know me to be, even if it wasn't on your schedule."

In the distance, Babe could hear the sound of a boat motoring through the water. Those on the bus ran off and to the water's edge. The two members of the team watched him tackle Seb, then passively stand doing nothing. Each adult had four children; they crossed the beach, racing toward the powerboat. Jarvis looked at Babe, who saluted him and waved them off.

"Seb, I drive," Babe ordered.

Babe pulled out his phone and called Trinity. "Mission went with only one mishap. My girl, I will keep my phone on me; I hope I can keep you apprised."

"Where are you? I thought you said Wednesday." She sounded panicked.

"Too long of a story, now. I'll tell Javier you send your greetings. I love you."

"Babe!" She cried into the phone. "Nooo!"

"It's okay, my girl. I'll call."

They pulled onto the property. Sounding like a whiny little girl, Seb said, "They'll never let you in. I should be driving."

"Bet you they will. One grand." Babe chuckled.

"Fuck you. You'll see."

The massive gate crept open. Babe pulled in. Then, the ornate iron gate opened. Babe drove to the entrance of the house. Javier stood outside waiting. "Welcome, my Marine friend." Seb was fit to be tied. "Seb, you owe the Captain a debt?" The younger man clenched his jaw in anger. His dark eyes burned with hatred. The Marine waved his hand laterally, saying Seb didn't owe a debt. "Are you certain?" Babe nodded, closing his eyes. "Very well. Let us pour a drink to the success of your venture. Do you realize you have cost me much money? Drugs are a one-time payout, but people, I can collect multiple times a day on one. That's a lot of dinero, yes?" Javier walked to the bar. "Have a seat. I have your brand, Glenlivet. I see you are married now. I hadn't heard. Congratulations." He handed Babe the glass. "Your clothes are still in the closet. We have an outing tomorrow."

Babe reclined a little in the chair, feeling relaxed and without trepidation. What it all came down to was if Javier wanted him dead, then he'd be dead. There was no point in worrying about it. "If you don't mind, I'll be having a shower and calling Trinity. When should I tell her I'll be home?"

Javier looked out of the window. "I had to ask myself, why didn't you kill Seb, join your amigos, and head home? I know you killed quite a few of my men; why not young Seb?" Babe had to think about it. Why didn't he?

"I'll tell you tomorrow. What time is the meeting, and am I a bodyguard again or something entirely different? Has Noir returned yet?" He ran his finger on the rim of the glass, looking into the amber swirl. The question Javier asked was one to contemplate. Was it because he was just a yes-man? It certainly wasn't his age; he'd killed younger. Seb wasn't attacking the kids, dragging them off, threatening to kill them; maybe that was why. "Does Seb partake in the kiddy porn or abuse personally?" Javier shook his head with a grin. "See, the others were coming after the kids, throwing them, being rough. Seb never went for any of them, not even the teenage girls. Perhaps there's the answer."

Javier turned toward Babe and spoke, "Be ready tomorrow at ten, and you might have to do what you do at the meeting." He walked toward the door, showing Babe out. Their conversation was over. "Seb is a kind, gentle soul." Babe passed through the door as Javier closed it. *Do what I do? What kind of answer was that? Then, like a flash, he remembered telling Trinity, I kill people. That's what I do, and anyone with any worldly savvy knows. Why else would Trey and Max ask? Why would Antoine ask if things were taken care of after the rape? That certainly wasn't a standard question one would ask an individual they didn't know and know well.*

He popped into the kitchen, grabbed a piece of fruit, and looked in the fridge. He was hungry. The cook walked into the kitchen, "Food, eat?"

"Por favor." The extent of his linguistic abilities was rather pathetic: si, bueno, bonita, por favor, gringo, dinero, and basic numbers. The cook prepared a hot plate of chicken and rice. He should be having stewed chicken and rice at Louie's. She had said rescuing the kids was important, but why didn't he run to the boat, and what the hell was the salute to Jarvis about? Did he want to see Javier again? The thoughts drummed through his head with each bite of food until the plate was empty.

The thoughtfulness followed him into the shower. He pictured Trinity's face, beautiful eyes, sexy lips, and tiny but perfect body; his body betrayed him and was rock hard. Once done in the shower, he padded into the room, opened the closet, and pulled out a pair of joggers. After getting comfortable on the sofa, he called Trinity.

"Hey, you. Now, what the hell is going on?" She asked, no longer panicky, more curious.

Babe told her about the rescue, the firefight, the bus, and the girl, everything in detailed minutia. He explained how he questioned why he hadn't killed Seb or run away and gotten on the boat. He told her how he felt a draw to return to Javier's when the truck passed it. There was no rhyme or reason.

"I think you need a friend. You've been encapsulated your whole life, and now your emotions are blossoming; you need someone who understands you and holds no judgment. You and I are besties, no doubt, but there's no one here that would get you. My dad might, but it might be awkward, and I wouldn't like it."

He interjected she was on a roll trying to save him, and she hadn't finished the diatribe. His girl could talk. "Your father already knows the kind of man I am; don't kid yourself."

She quipped, "Maybe so, but back to my list. Trey and Max aren't options, nor are my brothers or Glenn. I feel you're not overly enamored by hanging with your military connections. No kidding, after the shit with

Tim Faraday. Whatever happened to him?" *Hmm, good question*; he'd have to ask Javier. "Jarvis's deal is different and, maybe, good once in a while, but he might not get you. From what you've told me about cartel man, he gets you. I hate you being away from me, but I'm not worried this time; it was your choice. Selfishly, I want you here. I miss you." He longed for her; it was bigger than anything he'd ever known. She owned his heart and soul. She briefed him on her progress in the bedroom and how he would be amazed. He responded with a chuckle. If he could see the floor, it would be a vast improvement. Trinity rattled on, reassuring him she'd keep things steady until he returned but for him to call and not leave her hanging. He loved everything about her, whether walking, playing in bed, sitting at Louie's, catching a word, peck, or wink on the run. She knew him better than anyone. Perhaps she was correct about Javier understanding him.

"Trinity, I'll be home soon, and I'll call. Until—I love you."

She sounded sad, "You better, boy. We need some us time."

"Roger, that." The call ended. The ache of being hungry paled in comparison to the hole left in his heart being miles apart. During the entire conversation, while in true form, verbose, and unyielding, he felt like there was something she wanted to say but was remaining silent. He'd pry in the next conversation.

Morning came, his phone buzzed. The voice was crisp and clear, "You okay, man?" Jarvis seemed concerned. "We got everyone where they needed to be, but there were a lot more than expected, which is a win. You certainly brought your A-game, but I don't understand why you went off with that dude; you could have demolished him and made it to the boat. I guess you have your reasons. Thanks for all you did. It ended up being fifty-four in all. That's big. Stay in touch and take care. Don't try to cut off the head of the snake alone, okay, big guy?"

"I had to do something; your team is balls out. Thank you for getting those people settled. I'll be in touch."

Babe rolled out of bed and headed to Javier's gym; indeed, it was the bomb. A couple of other people were working out, neither in good form. He could feel their eyes scoping him, watching his every move. He loaded up the weights on the barbell. They observed, not even trying to conceal their curiosity. When he started his routine, they chattered back and forth, obviously impressed by the gringo. Once he finished with the free weights, carefully returning everything to its place, he did his hundred chin-lifts, but crunches still pulled at the mending wound, topping him out at fifty. There wasn't enough time for a run, so he returned to his suite, showered, and dressed casually—black joggers, a tee shirt, and running shoes. Javier hadn't lied; all the clothes purchased for him were as he'd left them, including the Henley with the bullet tear; they laundered the blood from it.

After a light breakfast of fruit and a bagel, he waited in the great room for Javier. Precisely at ten, the man entered, followed by Seb. They conversed, the younger man pointing to Babe, obviously annoyed and feeling slighted. Seb didn't understand it was for his protection. If the Marine got killed, it was no sweat off his balls. Seb broke off and went to the kitchen, probably to sulk, Babe deduced.

"Where are we going, and what do you want from me? It must be crystal clear if I'm to do a job well." Babe followed close behind.

"I have two meetings; both should be without incident. You make a statement by your presence. It is not like last time when I was in negotiations. These are more social, keeping the blood off the streets." The car was waiting for them. When the driver opened the door, Babe saw an elaborate wine and fruit basket on the seat. *Odd.*

On the way, Javier went through a comprehensive schedule dotted with intel on the players and a scant history. Javier said they were going to the home of Manny Lopez's widow first. "The speculation is the sister of Mateo Moreno," Javier crossed himself, "out of retribution for the assassination, killed Manny. At one time, I was close to DeDe Moreno." He crossed himself twice. "She was the most attractive woman in the world, but ice ran through her veins. As a young man, I jumped through hoops for her attention, if you understand my meaning. Mateo looked the other way. Bonita." *Okay, so Javier was banging his best friend's sister. Got it.*

"Then, we are meeting some Federales. Even though they are on my payroll, I do not doubt they are on the payroll of others. They are a most corrupt and greed-filled people; it's a game of who pays the highest bribe. As Americans say, 'What have you done for me lately?' You are an unfamiliar face, and they will have no information about you. It'll spook them." He raised his eyebrows as punctuation. "They will keep their distance, demanding you to stay away from the table, but I will say no. If they become unruly, take out the closest one to you, and it'll take them by surprise. The more impressive the show, the better—they eat up dramatics. Everyone will draw their weapon, but it's all machismo." *I smell bullshit.*

Javier continued, smooth as silk, "Unfortunately, one of their men was executed in yesterday's fiasco. I told you you've cost me much money, for that I should order your execution, but last we met, you told me your plans to free my acquisitions. I am to blame for not moving them. Therefore, it is on me; besides, I like you. You are a strong adversary. I like a challenging opponent."

The whole thing was a farce. These meetings were the exact opposite of Javier's plan. He was setting Babe up and punishing him for the raid and rescue. Before the driver or Javier could comprehend the situation, Babe had the switchblade from his sock up against the boss's throat, digging the point against his carotid. "Here's what I think is going on. You are banking on a Federale, blowing me away. Why the pretense? You could have shot me last night. An associate asked me point-blank why I didn't disable Seb. It was out of respect for you, and now you set me up for execution." Javier shouted something to the driver. "Any slam of the brakes, swerve in steering, and this point will slice your carotid, and within minutes, you will bleed out."

Javier put his hands in the air, "I swear on the lives of my children I have no intention of killing you. What makes you think such a thing?" He sounded sincere, but Babe knew he was setting something in motion.

"Nothing, nothing, I swear is going on to do with you. I have business to discuss with them. They will probably send some women in for your entertainment. I know you are not interested, but play along, or at least smile." *I'm in the car; either I slice his throat or see what comes next. Is this the life I want?* Jarvis's question ran through his mind. Why did he want to see Javier? What was the point? Nonetheless, he was on the way to some widow's house and then, from the description, a whorehouse run by crooked Federales. *Peachy.* He put the knife away.

The car turned up a long driveway—beautiful gardens of flowers framed on either side. Stopping, the driver opened the door for Javier; Babe got out the other side. When the door opened, he could see a beautiful woman. Conjuring thoughts of Manny's widow, he envisioned a stout older woman, still in mourning black, like somebody's grandmother. The creature at the door was nothing close to the image he had formed. She embraced Javier, "It has been so long since I've seen you," she purred. "How is your wife? And children? Who do we have here?" She put her arm out to Babe.

"Hello, ma'am. I'm—"

Javier cut in, "This is my good friend, Captain Vicarell; he is a United States Marine only here for a short visit." She smiled politely at him. The way she was eyeing him made him feel uncomfortable. He made a point to play with the band on his left hand. It was duly noted. Javier took the basket from the driver and handed it to her. "A small gesture to let you know we think of you and are but ten minutes away. You should visit sometime. My wife and her sister travel extensively, but I know they would like to have you over for lunch." *So suave, Javier,* Babe thought. *Yes, the women are away often; come play.*

They sat on the back veranda enclosed by stone arches overlooking a beautiful pool and yard, not quite the splendor of Javier's but fabulous nonetheless. Her English, while broken, was far better than his Spanish;

thus, Javier would translate here and there. Two teenagers entered the room, griping and chastising each other or some familial discourse. She boldly corrected them and sent them off. "They were so small when my husband disappeared. They never found his body." She shook her head with saddened eyes. On the lamp table, she had a family portrait. Babe couldn't help but think the woman obviously married him for money and status because his girth was close to his stature. She was beautiful. All the women he'd seen in Javier's life were Latin goddesses.

The conversation went on for another thirty or forty minutes. Manny's widow opened the fruit and wine basket. From Babe's line of vision, he saw Javier had filled the bottom with stacks of money rather than the usual shredded fill. It was time to leave; she politely walked them to the door, gave Javier a congenial hug, and grabbed Babe by the arm, pulling him close to her body. "It was a pleasure to meet you, Captain." *More Latino heat.* Javier grinned.

They climbed into the car. "She was hot for you. I saw how she rubbed her nipples on your arm. Can you believe that gorgeous woman was married to Manny Fat Fuck? He was a spoiled child, as a man as well. There is no denying those are his children; the resemblance is striking. Hopefully, they will keep a decent weight like their mother, but Manny was always rounder than tall.

It was the next stop where Babe anticipated fireworks and would have to be tightly tuned. Switchblade hidden again in his sock, he was as prepared as possible. The concrete block building, painted the color of red clay, was surrounded by a wall to match. The gates were open, ready for them.

Two armed guards stood at the door, followed them inside, then remained on either side of the door. If they smiled, surely their faces would crack, such dour individuals. Upon entering the building, the bar was the first welcome area, with chaise lounges scattered along the walls and tables in the center. To Babe's disbelief, a man entered from another room with arms open and welcoming until he saw him. He dressed in audacious attire like a matador or theatre personality. His suit was bright red and sequined, rather shocking to Babe. His smile, in an instant, turned grave when he saw Babe. In Spanish, he must have complained or inquired about the stranger and why he was there. Javier answered quickly, and both men chuckled. He snapped his fingers, and three scantily clad women entered the room. They were not Latin goddesses—more like rode hard and put back wet. The barmaid entered. She was beautiful despite two carved scars vertically incised upon her face. Her outfit covered her body. "Sir," the Liberace impersonator spoke, "Which one of the ladies would you like to spend time with?" He posed with his hand on his hip and a smirk of a smile. *Cheesedick.*

Babe pointed to the barmaid. The host raised an eyebrow and shook his head no. "I'll pay double."

"But sir, she has," and he formed his hand along the side of his face, addressing the scars.

"Yes, a beautiful but scarred face provides a welcoming and tighter pussy." He thought Javier's mouth was about to hit the floor, but Babe kept a deadpan expression. "I want her." The man did not want Babe to have her, and the Marine had a good idea why. She had tried to get away, and he punished her. What other scars might she bear? This was the kind of shit that pissed him off, turning on his rage. He grabbed the woman by the arm, bringing her into the back room and drawing the curtain.

He put his finger to his lips, indicating she stayed quiet. "English?" She nodded. "Where else are you hurt?" She opened her blouse; they had branded her nipples. "I am not going to do anything, but we must act, do you understand?" She closed her eyes and nodded. She lay on a velvet bedspread and wrapped her legs around him. He nodded and went through the motions. They both performed a most convincing act. "Did Luis, sparkle-suit, do this?" She shook her head no. A man entered from a room to the rear; he had not seen the man before. She nodded. He winked at her.

The man gargled a laugh. "You want to make her wild on your dick?" From behind his back, he brought out a branding iron. The man couldn't have played it more perfectly for Babe. He acted like he pulled out of the woman and zipped his pants. The man dropped his pants to his knees, stroked himself a few times, and leaned in to enter her. Babe took the man's legs out from under him and grabbed the branding iron crushing it on his engorged cock. The pain sucked the breath out of him so that he couldn't yell at first; not wasting a second, Babe crushed his windpipe, and his eyes nearly popped out of their orbit. The clunk of the still red hot iron hitting the floor brought sparkle suit into the room. He gasped in horror and started to run away. Three strides and Babe was on top of the guy, snapped his neck. One of the gunmen at the door opened up. He held the dead man in front of him and slung his knife across the room into the heart of the other gunman. Javier had thrown himself over the bar, pulled out his gun, and took out the remaining gunman. The person behind the bar had wet himself and stood shaking. The three harlots had already returned to their waiting room, and he felt sure they were trying to find a place to hide from the gunshots.

"What the fuck did you do?" Javier quizzed.

"Sent a message. Go, go, go." He grabbed the girl, Javier had enough time to glance at the man with the branded cock, but hauled ass to the car, and they spun out, heading to Casa Garcia. "Now, what the fuck did I do? I had a feeling the scars on her face were not the only ones. The man I used the iron on had branded her breasts, and I don't know what else. She needs plastic surgery. I know a plastic surgeon if you send her home with me."

Javier looked closer at the girl. "I know her. Olivia?" The girl nodded. Javier's head dropped to his chest.

Tears formed in her eyes, "Sebastian?"

"With me," he answered. "When we get to my house, you can freshen up and then tell Seb, me, and my friend what happened." She nodded with a faint smile.

"You want to know what happened, Javier?" Babe asked with a

roughness to his voice. "She was abducted, forced into prostitution, tried to escape, and punished for the attempt. Babe could feel the flush of anger on his face. The heat had moved up his neck and chest. The bodies they left at the Federale whorehouse didn't quell his rage. He wanted to fight the whole world.

They were almost at the house when Javier spoke. "She's a local girl; I don't get it. Why didn't anyone report it?" He was genuinely perplexed.

"Those closest to home are low-hanging fruit. It is happening everywhere. As you told me once, it is a hundred-billion-dollar industry. Remember, you explained how it was a better investment than drugs because it wasn't a one-and-done, but something to turn over and over in a day."

Javier cleared his throat, "It is." He looked out the window. Was he having second thoughts? Is this maybe why Mateo hadn't wanted to get into trafficking? Babe could see Javier's reflection; he saw the pain, disgust, and self-loathing.

The driver pulled into Casa Garcia. Javier called someone. "Come out to the car."

In a minute, maybe two Seb came out the door. Javier got out of the car, followed by Olivia. Babe exited the other side and walked around the vehicle.

Seb's eyes widened like saucers, tears trickling down his cheeks. "Olivia, oh, my God. Where have you been? I looked and looked. I asked everyone, but no one knew where you were." He touched the side of her face and ran his fingers along the scars, shaking his head. "Who did this?"

Javier interrupted. "Let's get her inside and cleaned up. I imagine she will be staying in your quarters, Seb?" He nodded and led her to the room, shortly to return. "The Marine knows the story. He was the one who freed her and eliminated the Federales. Her captors are dead."

The three sat while Babe filled him in on what he knew about her abuse. He mentioned she was probably trying to escape to find Seb when they located and punished her. The Marine explained he requested her instead of one of the prostitutes with no intention of having any of them. Babe figured there were more scars on her body and was right, but the man who hurt her had felt his wrath with a branding iron, but it was her story to tell.

Whether decisions or business plans changed was not in his wheelhouse. All Babe knew was he wanted to get home to Trinity and a boring but happy life. No, he didn't need the tension of wondering when he'd need to dodge a bullet, fight for his life, or exterminate the person going for him. Babe packed all the clothes Javier had bought for him. He wouldn't need them anymore; he was going home, never to return to Cartagena. As the jet took off and the tropics faded away, he was excited to return to NOLA, Trinity, the boys, Gunner, and Louie's.

LET THE GOOD TIMES ROLL

The air travel home gave him ample time to think about his life. Did he have an end game, and if so, what was it? Marriage had come up, but he wasn't sure he was the marrying kind, nor did he think Trinity was. There was no need to evaluate the love; it was as perfect as possible. The dye was pretty much cast with the three boys; preference or not, they were his. Rune's financial advisor had set him up with their legal team, where he could speak lawyer to lawyer. He always found it odd people were shocked to find out he had a Law Degree and chose to be a Marine. It's funny what held importance to some people. Jack Kennedy, his wrestling coach, referenced the order of priority on many occasions: God, Country, and Family. The standard was God, Family, and Country, but Jack Kennedy saw it differently.

While Babe had held many of the values of his coach, somehow, he'd skipped the God part. Coach Kennedy didn't speak to him about his home life, but there was an understanding in the silence. There was no need to whine to anybody about his abusive, asshole sperm donor; nothing would change the course. The end game on that one had not played out yet. There had been moments when he contemplated finding the man, but as quickly as the idea came into focus, he erased it for another time.

Looking out the window and catching a glimpse of his reflection reminded him of watching Javier's expression in the window. Was there a twinkle of hope in him changing ways? Probably not; he had too much on the line, and it would be hard for most people to walk away from a dynasty resurrected. The man had it all—a loving wife, children, a beautiful home, and all the creature comforts one could want. The way he lavishly threw money around as though it were nothing could pass as nauseating. The absurd amount of clothing he had provided him twice was over the top. The suite and rooms he had at the resort in Pensacola and Miami had to be a fortune. He didn't think twice about acquiring new cars and the sheer fact he had multiple pilots on standby, yet he was a prisoner to his lifestyle. Ideas pinged from one to the next without rhyme or reason, bringing Babe to the point of lunacy, like chasing a rabbit down a hole. He needed to compartmentalize his life and keep every aspect in its place—neat, organized, and Marine standard. What would be next on his dance card?

Zoom, and he was on another ninety-degree avenue. How long did Trinity plan on working at Louie's? He couldn't see her being one of those older craggle-faced bartenders with too much rouge, blue eye shadow, and over-done painted lips with a cigarette balancing on her bottom lip. But, could he see her in a soccer mom outfit, sitting on the PTA, driving a Suburban with a carful of whiny kids? Kids, indeed. He had nieces and or nephews he'd never seen, hell, a brother he'd never met. He remembered how uncomfortable he'd felt at the barbecue with Trinity's big family. Was that his future, grilling burgers and dogs, sipping brewskies on a Sunday afternoon after Mass?

So many questions and no answers—as a Marine, it was a world he couldn't function in, not by a long shot. His life had to have rules, order, a place for everything, and everything in its place. Behind the mayhem of war were the hard and fast rules; it was the only way they could have grasped the missions at hand. He longed to be like the people on the construction site, but would that force him down a tube of insanity? He wasn't built to be an average stiff.

Babe's stomach dropped as the altitude changed. It had been a flight of what-ifs and maybes, and within the next twenty minutes, he'd be hailing a cab to see his lady. He had no words to express the flight of nonstop random postulations.

What day was it? He left with Jarvis's team on Monday, rescued the victims onto boats that evening, and had the encounter with Seb, but it was into the wee hours of Tuesday. He hit the bed, then re-grouped that afternoon. Javier had the widow and Federale meeting on Wednesday, or was it Thursday? What a fucking nightmare that was; his gut served him well when he asked for the girl with the scarred face. Sick motherfuckers. To think she had been Seb's intended. What an odd set of circumstances. It was strange how things worked out. He checked his phone; it was Wednesday, and by the time he got to Louie's, it'd be midnight or after, so technically, it was almost Thursday.

To his surprise, a black SUV waited on the tarmac as they came to a stop. Nobody was supposed to know where he was, yet a car awaited him. Maybe it was waiting for the pilots. It felt all too familiar. Then he saw her. Trinity was standing next to the vehicle. Given her petite stature, it made the SUV look massive. Babe felt his emotions tumbling through his gut like sagebrush in the western desert. Did his questions really require answers? She was all he needed and wanted.

As he disembarked, she ran toward the jet. He scooped her up in his arms. Trinity kissed him over and over. "You're home, at last. With all your missions completed, for now, I expect to have your undivided attention. I want every detail, Babe Vicarelli. We have some stuff to talk about after I hear all the juicy bits." He opened the car door for her.

"Yes, ma'am. All the juicy bits," and laughed.

She watched him walk around the vehicle and slide in; putting it in Drive, he took off. "So, your friend Jarvis called me. He sounds nice. I had already spoken to you, but he didn't know; it was thoughtful that he called to let me know where you were. I'm happy everything went well, and you're home safe. So, start from when you left home."

The entire way to her place, he told her about the rescue mission, including the firefight. He told her about the team and how he was impressed—then the weirdness of pity concerning Seb. "I don't know why I wanted to go to Javier's; I didn't have to. I could have taken care of him," he snapped his fingers. "Even though he's an insecure little dick, he didn't deserve to get hurt or die. Javi was his usual self—aloof, arrogant, and sophisticated. The guy glides when he walks. You'd more than likely think he was handsome. He's got a velvety Latin voice. He could probably say anything, and it would sound appealing to a woman." He then told her about the widow, the hidden money, and then a brief graze about the Federales.

"N-no, sir. Babe, I know you well; something went down with the" using air quotes, "Federales. Don't try to play that game." He started to unpack the meeting. "Whorehouse?" Her voice went up an octave. "They expected you to go with one of the whores?" He nodded. "And so what did you do?" Tongue in cheek, he responded, when in Rome. Her jaw dropped in disbelief, but he told her about the barmaid with the scars on her face and his suspicions, especially when they didn't want him to pay for her.

"She spoke a little English, enough to understand I did not want her services. I had a feeling she had more scars, and she did." He explained about the branding. Trinity gasped. "I asked her if Mr. Sparkle Suit was the one who hurt her. She said no, but then a heartless-looking bastard walked in from the back, and she barely nodded, but enough for me to tell. She had her blouse open, and skirt hiked around her; anyway, she knew we were pretending. The man slurred some crude remarks, and I moved for him to take a turn. He had the branding iron, planning to use it on her. When he lowered his pants, I hooked his ankles, making him stumble onto his back and branded his cock and ball sack." She gasped again. "I took out three, and Javier took out one. We ditched out of the place with the girl.

Odd luck, the girl had been Seb's fiancee until she went missing." Trinity had tears trickling down her face.

"Vic, you coulda been killed. I guess the guy, Seb, now doesn't act like a jerk to you. Fate is a weird thing. If you had gotten on the boat with Jarvis, then the girl would've never been saved; now she and Seb can be together." She snuggled into him, stretching the seat belt. "See, you are a superhero. My superhero." She kissed his arm.

Traffic was light given the hour. Babe and Trinity made it to Hotel Noelle, and he pulled into the parking garage. "Who's car is this? Big Paul's?" She nodded. He walked around the vehicle, and she slid into his arms as she lowered onto the pavement.

"Ya know, he acts like he hates me and tells me I'm a pain in his ass, but I think he likes me and thinks I'm funny. We have some household things to discuss, but let's get you settled."

He threw his luggage on the bed. Trinity opened the case. "Where in the hell did you get all these clothes? They are nice; I mean, look at the brands. You spent a fortune." She held up a shirt. "This shirt alone was two hundred dollars." She flew through the clothes, commenting the entire time. "Have you ever owned so many pairs of pants or shoes? Holy shit, Babe. You spent a boatload."

He lay against the headboard, watching her with a grin; he'd never seen her so animated and found it amusing. "I didn't buy any of them. Javier bought them, and he had already bought the same amount, but we had to leave Miami and our possessions behind. We had to dig out fast, balls to the wall." At the bottom of the case was the Bible Javi's son had given him. He knew there would be questions.

"And this? Do tell." She glanced at him with curiosity.

"I like Psalms, Samuel, and King David. He and I have much in common other than he was a man after God's heart, not a Satan spawn, but make no mistake, he was one tough motherfucker. Come here." Babe picked her up and put her on his lap, intertwining his hands with hers. He took each and kissed them one at a time. "So tiny and perfect. I see you still have the pink band on. I'm glad." She started to get up to hang his clothes. "Stay. The room looks amazing, and I'll hang those when we're finished. Now, what housekeeping measures do we need to discuss? Can they wait?" His eyes twinkled with sass.

She stretched her arms over her head and groaned, "I suppose." She peeled her top off, showing off her bra. He grinned. She stood on the bed and pulled her yoga pants down. He cocked his head, watching the show.

"A bra? Stretchy pants? A new look for you. Looks good. You look radiant. I guess you are happy to see me; you're glowing."

She nodded, pointing to his shirt and jeans, clearing her throat. He got the message loud and clear and peeled off his clothing.

"Today is Thursday," he said with determination as he walked out of the bedroom. The princess was still sleeping as he worked out in the dining room corner. Pull-ups, situps, and free weights first; he hustled Gunner, preparing for a run. "Come on, boy." He took off around the block. It was unusually brisk, but the cool air felt good against his face. What an odd set of circumstances had befallen him. *Civilian life is not for me*, he thought, *but what is?* He passed by Conti, where the demolition was in the works. The office trailer from the old job site had moved to the new project, parked half in and half out of the street. The men had constructed a fence around the property to protect passersby or keep out thieves. He opened the door. "Good morning, Glenn." His boss had a look of surprise.

"Boy, are you a sight for sore eyes. Trinity told me you did a search and rescue operation. Wow. That's intense. I saw a trailer for a new movie on television about human trafficking, and then I heard you're doing the same thing. Holy crap. What was it like?" Babe sat for a few minutes, sketching how sad and horrific the situation was. He briefly mentioned he and Trinity had three boys they'd taken into their home. "Trinity's place in Lakeview?"

"No, sir. I have a generational family house. My grandfather left it to me. We have a caretaker who watches over the boys and runs the place. You'd swear she was military." He coughed a laugh.

Glenn asked, "So whatcha think about Miss Trinity?"

"She looks great and has been a trooper through all the weirdness I brought to the table." Glenn smiled but remained quiet. "I gotta run by the place and change for work, but I'll be back."

Glenn bent over the blueprints. "Okay, Vicarelli. See you in a while."

By the time he and Gunner returned, Trinity was up and had hung all of Babe's clothes in the closet. "Look at you, all domestic," he teased.

She gave him a sideways glance, "Um, something like that. Babe, we need to talk." He sat on the armrest of the sofa with a hand towel, wiping the sweat from his face. She pulled her nightshirt over her head and stood before him naked.

His eyes shifted in question. "Okay, I get you missed me, but wouldn't it be better to strip in the bedroom?"

"No, the light isn't as good as it is in here. You don't notice anything?" He turned his hands up. "You know my little bitty titties? Well?" He glanced at her breasts; they were definitely fuller.

"If you're trying to tell me you got a boob job, it's your body, girl, do what you want. I love you no matter what. You're beautiful." She rolled her eyes.

Standing with her hand on her hip, she looked at him. "For fuck's sake, no, I didn't get a boob job!" She turned to the side. "Notice anything?" Babe scoped her body, head tilting from side to side. His eyes rounded wide; yes, he saw and understood finally. *What to say?* "And? Happy?

Angry? Double-timing it out the door, or excited? I'm thrilled and, yes, pregnant. You ready to be a dad, big man?" He stood with a gobsmacked grin and slowly nodded. *Do I, I don't know. Crap.*

"I'm gonna be a dad. Give me a minute to digest this." He looked back at her with tears frosting his eyes. "I've been trying to figure out what I want to do—I'm not a regular stiff; I don't play by the rules because there isn't a playbook. I guess we've answered what I'm gonna do. Now I know exactly. I'm gonna be a dad. Fuckin-A!"

For more adventure, tip-toeing on the edge, and flirting with the past all in a New Orleans tale, join Babe, Trinity, Trey, Max, and Gunner in *The Inevitable Lie*, the fourth book in the **FIT THE CRIME** series. If you enjoyed *The Impossible Lie*, please visit my website, corinnearrowood.com. Be sure to register to receive monthly newsletters and the occasional freebie. Take a moment to go to the site of purchase and leave a review; I love hearing from y'all.

As always, I wish you love.

—Corinne Arrowood

Many Thanks...

Doug Arrowood, my husband, my heart, my love, and the one that keeps me sane, thank you for reeling me in when I go too far out on the ledge. Your positive spirit and encouraging words pump me up when I need them; you do it without even knowing. Your driving spirit keeps me in touch with reality and the possibilities.

Kaye, Kristen, Nick, John, and #5. Y'all make it so easy to be your mom. Your support fills my heart. Please keep spreading the word and coming to my events. It gives me an extra boost when I see y'all at the release parties and signings.

Riley, Brennon, Kerrison, Knox, Kressley, Ari, Kambrey, Téa, Krew, Avery, Andrew, Cole, and Willa...your magic creates magic in me, and your laughter ignites my laughter. Thanks for the love and affirmation.

Paige Brannon Gunter, my forever editor, as long as you'll have me. You spur me to write better. I love your suggestions and the sensitivity you have for all my characters. You keep it real for me, and yes, I know, thanks to you, not everyone likes chocolate ice cream.

K.N. Faulk, thank you for the time you have spent with me and for loving my characters. I know you are sensitive to my feelings and artistic temperament (weenie with flowers), but I appreciate you pointing out discrepancies. You keep me on my toes. Merci.

Julie Agan, your input regarding the life of a Marine and the repercussions as that of a mom of a Marine have given me an insight I otherwise would not have had. Thank you for sharing with me.

Cyrus Wraith Walker, your creativity and patience with me are astounding. You are always there to answer my questions or develop ideas I hadn't considered. The cover keeps getting better and better. Thank you, Artistic Guru.

With heartfelt gratitude and appreciation, thank you to the members of our Armed Forces for the sacrifice and service they have so freely given to protect our country and way of life. We can enjoy freedom because of you and your family's dedication, sacrifice, and courage.

Huge thank you to my readers who are taking this journey with me. Your support is everything. Please continue to spread the word, and thank you for your praise. You know how to make a girl feel like a million bucks. Here's to book four; be on the lookout. Cheers!

Other Books by the Author
Censored Time Trilogy
A Quarter Past Love (Book I)
Half Past Hate (Book II)
A Strike Past Time (Book III)

Friends Always
A Seat at the Table
PRICE TO PAY
The Presence Between

Fit the Crime Series
The Innocence Lie (Book I)
The Identity Lie (Book II)

Be On the Look Out for...
Leave No Doubt
The Inevitable Lie (Book IV of the Fit The Crime series)

Visit my website, corinnearrowood.com, and register to win freebies
Reviews are appreciated

About The Author

According to Me

Local girl to the core. There's nowhere on earth like New Orleans! I am still very much in love with my husband of over thirty-five years, handsome hunk, Doug. I'm a Mom, Nana, and great-Nana. (four kids, thirteen grands, three great-grands) Favorite activities include hanging with the hubs, watching grandkids' games and activities, hiking, reading, and traveling. I am addicted to watching The Premier League, particularly Liverpool—The real football—married to a Brit; what can I say? Living my best life writing and playing with my characters and their stories. I'm a Girl Raised In The South (G.R.I.T.) Perhaps the most important thing about me is my faith in God. All of my characters, thus far, have opened a closed heart to an open one filled with Light. Some take longer than others.

According to the Editors

Born and raised in the enchanting city of New Orleans, the author lends a flavor of authenticity to her books and the characters that come to life in stories of love, lust, betrayal, and murder. Her vivid style of storytelling transports the reader to the very streets of New Orleans with its unique sights, smells, and intoxicating culture.

9 781962 837019